Murder at the Opera House
Large Print Edition

A Lady Marjorie Snellthorpe Mystery Book 1

Dawn Brookes

Dawn Brookes
Publishing

This novel is entirely a work of fiction. The names, characters and incidents portrayed are the work of the author's imagination except for those in the public domain. Any resemblance to actual persons, living or dead, is entirely coincidental. Although real-life places are depicted in settings, all situations and people related to those places are fictional.

Paperback Edition 2021
Standard Paperback ISBN: 978-1-913065-57-7
Large Print Paperback: 978-1-913065-60-7

Cover Images adapted from Adobe Stock Images:
Cluj Opera House
Elderly lady in foreground
Cover Design: John and Janet

Chapter 1

Edna Parkinton stood waving her ample arms in the air, yelling at the top of her voice. "Over here, Marge!"

Seeing Edna in the centre of the concourse at Luton Airport making an exhibition of herself, Marjorie Snellthorpe was already regretting her decision to join the woman for a holiday. Her wretched cousin-in-law persisted in calling her *Marge,* despite knowing how much Marjorie hated her name being shortened. If she was going to survive the next fortnight, Marjorie would need to make every effort not to rise to the bait. But, with this being just the start of their trip to Romania, it wasn't going to be easy. She could have kicked herself for her stupidity.

When Edna had telephoned a few months earlier, she had been on her best behaviour. The sole purpose of the call, of course, was to persuade Marjorie to join her on a Danube River cruise from Bucharest to Budapest with various stops along the way. Edna had promised she would endeavour not to annoy her; a promise, experience told Marjorie, the woman was incapable of keeping. Marjorie inhaled a deep breath before joining Edna. Thankfully, most people were too busy checking on their own flights to pay too much attention to them.

"Hello, Edna."

"Hiya, Marge." Edna leaned down as if to hug her, but Marjorie backed away.

"I hope I haven't kept you waiting."

Edna accepted the rebuff but wasn't easily put off. "I see you can't manage your own suitcases. Mind you, if I'd seen this one, I might have been tempted to feign the helpless female." Then, she had the audacity to blink flirtatious false lashes before winking at the handsome young porter assisting Marjorie with her luggage.

"Oh, do stop it. You're too old for this kind of behaviour, despite the wig and the Plaster of Paris hiding your face." Edna had suffered from alopecia since having chemotherapy treatment for cancer. She was one of the rare people whose hair had never grown back. Marjorie knew she was being unkind, but she couldn't help herself. The woman riled her so much.

"It's me favourite wig," Edna was now addressing the porter as she touched up her bright red hair, "but I have an extensive collection – including blonde, if you prefer blondes."

The porter chuckled politely, clearly not knowing how to handle the force that was Edna Parkinton. *But then, who does?* thought Marjorie. Before Edna embarrassed either of them any further, Marjorie turned to him.

"Where to now?"

"You check in over there," he answered, rushing ahead of them, pulling her suitcase and travel bag along as though they were feathers.

"Blimey! He's in a hurry, ain't he?" said Edna.

"I wonder why," muttered Marjorie under her breath.

The two women followed the swarthy porter and joined the queue at the check-in desk. They were flying with an airline Marjorie had never heard of before, but it was the only one that offered a nonstop flight to Cluj-Napoca where they would begin their holiday. Once they had checked in, Marjorie gave the porter a generous tip. It was the least she could do after he had suffered ten minutes in Edna's company while they waited to show their tickets to an unfriendly burly woman at the desk.

Apart from being fifteen minutes late boarding and having to put up with Edna complaining once she realised they would be sitting separately, Marjorie was pleased to be seated on the aeroplane. She had purposely advance-booked a front seat, which meant she could at least have a little peace during the flight. The plane trip went without mishap, except for Marjorie, and the rest of the passengers, being subjected to Edna's loud voice rattling off tales of her years working on the stage to whoever had the misfortune to be sitting next to her.

It was hot and sultry when Marjorie disembarked. Nevertheless, she was feeling smug that she had managed to escape almost three hours of Edna's endless chatter and could now leave the aircraft ahead of her. Another ploy that was working well. She looked up at the sign: Avram Iancu International Airport. It was named after a mid-nineteenth century Romanian revolutionary according to the literature she had read during the flight.

While Marjorie was waiting in the baggage area, Edna finally caught up with her.

"Here she is. This is my cousin, Marge. Marge, this is Fred. He's on the same tour we are."

A slight bald-headed man wearing a smart blue suit with a blue checked shirt gave Marjorie a shy smile. His confused grey eyes told her he was clearly overawed by Edna.

She took pity on him, holding out her hand. “I’m Marjorie, Marjorie Snellthorpe and no-one calls me Marge apart from Edna, who incidentally is my cousin-*in-law*. She’s my late husband’s cousin.”

The reserved man shook her hand after wiping his forehead with a handkerchief. “Actually, I’m Frederick, Frederick Mackworth. I haven’t been called Fred since leaving school, and that was some time ago.” He cast a cautious glance over at Edna as if in fear for his life, but she was already barging her way to the front of the baggage carousel, searching for their suitcases.

Marjorie would never tell her so, but having Edna along to track down her hefty suitcase turned out to be useful, as it was stuck behind someone else’s luggage. She watched as Edna, determined not to let it escape, bulldozed her way past a family, calling out to a tall young man.

“Oi! Don’t just stand there. Grab that case.”

Who would dare refuse the crazed woman with fiery red hair? The man did as instructed.

Frederick was able to retrieve his baggage with much less drama. He smiled at Marjorie.

“Your cousin-in-law has quite the presence, doesn’t she?”

Rolling her eyes, Marjorie replied, “Yes, she leaves an impression, there’s no doubting that. How are you getting to the hotel?”

“I was going to get a taxi. Would you like to share?”

“That makes sense. I’m not familiar with the customs of Romanian taxi drivers, and it’s always good economy to split the costs where one can.” She didn’t want to mention she was also worried about Edna embarrassing her further by arguing over fares.

“It’s my first time here, too. Shame they didn’t put on a bus for us, but then, I’m not sure how many people are meeting in Cluj and how many are joining us in Bucharest.”

Marjorie couldn't quite work out Frederick's accent. She thought West Country; Bristol, perhaps.

"I believe there will be ten of us here. Edna would have been far happier spending a few days on the Black Sea coast before joining the party in Bucharest, but I was keen to visit the opera when I saw the alternative. Speaking of Edna, where has she got to?"

"She's chatting to a tall man on the other side of the concourse."

Marjorie turned, hoping Edna hadn't left her suitcase unguarded while chatting up her latest conquest in trousers. At least Marjorie had her hand baggage containing all her valuables with her.

"Oh yes, I see her now. I recognise him. He was on the Amsterdam cruise we took earlier in the year. Now, what was his name? It'll come to me..." Marjorie observed Edna chortling loudly with the tall, distinguished-looking man whose dyed brown hair, she recalled, was in part a toupee.

"I remember now! Horace, Horace Tyler. He has an avionics firm or some such thing. Semi-retired, but I believe he still oversees it."

Frederick seemed slightly disappointed that Edna's attention was being taken up by Horace Tyler. *What is it about that woman?* She certainly had a penchant for attracting the opposite sex, even at eighty. Mind you, Horace was no spring chicken, despite Marjorie recalling he had a liking for younger women. He had turned out to be all right in the end, though, and at least his presence would keep Edna out of her hair.

Marjorie spied her suitcase next to Edna's. "I think we had better retrieve Edna and my luggage if we want to get to the hotel in time for a bite to eat. I can never eat aeroplane food."

"It's perhaps as well as there wasn't any," Frederick chuckled. He had a genuine, open smile. "Budget airlines don't go in for those extras. I only flew with them for the direct flight."

"Same here," said Marjorie. "It was quite comfortable, though, and we got here in one piece. That's the main thing."

Marjorie and Frederick joined Edna and Horace, who were laughing at something Edna had said.

"Look who's here, Marge," Edna said, sending a teasing grin Horace's way.

"Yes, fancy." Marjorie suspected Horace was another reason for Edna's keenness to come on this particular trip. "Hello again," she said, holding out her hand.

"Hello, Lady Marjorie. Good to see you again. New boyfriend, I see." Horace raised a trimmed eyebrow. Edna snorted.

Feeling herself stiffen, Marjorie replied, "We've just met. This is Frederick Mackworth. Frederick, this is Horace Tyler."

Horace shook Frederick's hand. "Good to meet you, Fred. As there's four of us, shall we share a taxi?" Horace and Edna were peas in a pod when it came to familiarity.

"*Fredrick*," Marjorie said pointedly, "and I had the same idea."

"Come on, then, we can get one just outside. Don't worry, I won't let them rip us off. I've been here many times on business."

Of course you have, thought Marjorie, remembering Horace was also a show-off.

The taxi journey to the hotel was a tight fit with Edna's suitcase, being the largest, having to join the passengers in the back seat, but the driver was pleasant and accommodating. He and Horace, who sat in the front seat, chatted about how much Cluj had changed since the revolution in 1989. The taxi driver spoke in broken English most of the time, but Horace seemed to be able to communicate in Romanian, switching languages at will.

On entering the luxurious Hotel Platinia, Marjorie immediately caught sight of Faith Weathers, a tour guide for the company they were booked with. Queen Cruises owned many subsidiaries, and Queen River and Land Tours was one of them. The parent company had developed expanded itineraries, or so the literature said, to incorporate inland tours as well as river and sea cruises.

Faith stood close to reception, ready to welcome them, passenger list and clipboard in hand. Marjorie paused to take in her surroundings. She had never been to Romania before, which was the only reason she had reluctantly agreed to accompany her irritating cousin-in-law. Despite herself, she was excited to be in a new place.

"Lady Marjorie! How nice to see you again," Faith's greeting was warm and her smile genuine, although Marjorie noticed her casting a wary glance Edna's way. "Good to see you too, Edna. It doesn't seem two minutes since we were sailing the Rhine."

"We're happy to be here. It wasn't a long flight, but there wasn't any food. If you could spare us the dead body this time, I'd appreciate it." Edna snorted loudly.

"Body? What body?" Frederick's eyes widened, creasing his forehead.

“Nothing to concern yourself with, Fred. There was an accident on the last trip we took, that’s all,” said Horace dismissively. “Some woman took a tumble down the stairs.”

Marjorie sensed Edna itching to argue the point and regale them with details about the murder of a guest at the hotel at the start of their last holiday, but Faith hastened the conversation on.

“You’re in room twenty-two, Edna, and you’re in thirty-six, Lady Marjorie. Here are your keys.” Faith handed them both envelopes containing key cards.

“Couldn’t you find rooms for us next door to each other?” Edna complained.

Faith shrugged her shoulders. “Sorry, we had to take what we were allocated.”

Marjorie mouthed a thank you, knowing Faith would have done her utmost to ensure a degree of separation between the two women.

Faith turned to Horace. “It’s a pleasure to have you with us again, Mr Tyler. Welcome to the Platinia, you’re in room forty-nine.”

“Thank you,” said Horace. “This is Fred, we met at the airport.”

Faith turned her attention to Frederick, and Marjorie heard her say he was in room twenty-three. Close to Edna, poor man.

“I’ve organised a private welcome buffet in the Picasso Conference Room,” said Faith. “Would you like me to have your luggage taken to your rooms?”

“That would be most kind,” said Marjorie, “I haven’t eaten since breakfast. Which way is the conference room?”

Faith called for a porter who appeared with a trolley. The luggage was already labelled, so Faith handed him a list with the room numbers and he loaded their suitcases onto the trolley before heading towards a service lift.

"I'll take you through to the Picasso myself. You're the final four. The other six came together and are already there."

They followed Faith to the conference room, where two tables had been covered with tablecloths. Other tables in the centre were laid out with a selection of food.

Marjorie had warmed to their guide on the previous holiday. Faith was prim and efficient, despite a weakness for the wrong type of man. She wore her dark brown hair in a ponytail and, like Edna, used a lot of makeup. Faith's, though, brought out the best in her, whereas Edna's sometimes made her complexion resemble a sponge cake that had spent too long in the open.

As she took in the details of the conference centre, Marjorie's musings were rudely interrupted. Her head spun around towards the racket coming from the only occupied table in the room.

Chapter 2

It was impossible not to notice the rowdy group of six people sitting around the table. They appeared to be bickering, to put it mildly.

"Those are your fellow guests," Faith sighed, her voice quiet. She then headed swiftly to the tables where a mass of food was elegantly presented. "Help yourselves to the buffet. It's just us, so eat as much as you like. Although, I'd save some room for dinner. You'll dine at six in the à la carte restaurant. After dinner, a minibus will transport us to the opera. We'll be leaving for the airport in the morning to board our flight to Bucharest. You'll find all the details in your itineraries."

"What itinerary?" quizzed Edna.

"Don't worry, I arranged for copies to be left in each of your rooms just in case anyone forgot to bring the ones sent with your booking," Faith explained.

"I've got mine right here," said Horace, tapping the inside breast pocket of his immaculately tailored grey suit.

"Me too," remarked Frederick. "Old habits die hard."

Marjorie noticed a faraway look in the unassuming man's brooding grey eyes. *I must find out more about Mr Frederick Mackworth,* she thought. Marjorie was about to say that her itinerary was in her handbag, but Edna had clearly had enough of this conversation.

"I'm starving," she declared, taking Horace's arm and leading him past Faith towards the buffet. "Come on, Marge," Edna called, as an afterthought.

It was Marjorie's turn to sigh, but she was then distracted by the heavy scraping of a chair across the floor. She turned to see a tall, buxom woman with jet black hair, looking to be in her late sixties, making a melodramatic exit.

"Mother, she didn't mean it." Another woman in her late thirties with a sandy brown bob chased after the departing diva.

"Looks like we've got some interesting company," Horace guffawed, helping himself to a large plateful of hors d'oeuvres.

"Shush, they'll hear you," said Marjorie, hoping to stop Edna from adding to her embarrassment, but it was too late.

"So what if they do? We can certainly hear them. They haven't stopped since we entered the room."

Marjorie's eyes pleaded with Faith, who thankfully took the hint.

"There's a wonderful meat selection on the other side of the table. Let me show you."

Horace and Edna followed their guide, clearly happy to add more food to their plates. Frederick was standing, frozen to the spot, staring at the door through which the stroppy woman and her daughter had just left.

"I don't mean to pry, but are you quite all right?" Marjorie asked.

Frederick jumped, shaking his head. "I'm sorry, it's just… oh, never mind… it was a long time ago." The demure man returned to the task at hand. His plate remained half empty because he and Marjorie had to wait for Edna and Horace to make room at the buffet, and neither of them seemed in any hurry to move away from the attractive platters laden with Romanian delicacies. Marjorie didn't feel she could press him any further, but hoped the tempestuous woman's presence wouldn't spoil his holiday.

Once they had all helped themselves to food, Marjorie and her companions sat at the second table not too far from the noisy crowd. Faith checked in on the four people remaining at the first table before coming to see if the diners at the second table were happy with their food and the arrangements for the evening.

"I bet you haven't eaten," said Marjorie, noticing a slight tremor in Faith's hands not dissimilar to how she herself reacted when in need of sustenance. "Why don't you get some food and join us?"

"Yes do, there's plenty left. I hate to see good food go to waste," said Horace encouragingly. "And, you can also give us the lowdown on..." he inclined his head towards the other group, who continued their arguing. Marjorie wondered if the disagreements were more out of habit than malice. She hoped so.

Faith smiled. "Thanks, I think I will join you, and I'll be happy to discuss any of the other holiday arrangements." She shot Horace a warning look, then went to fill a plate.

"That's me told," said Horace. "We'll get no gossip from her now."

"Quite right too," said Marjorie. She lowered her voice, "Especially as the subject matter is so close."

Edna cackled. "It'll all be revealed soon enough. They're hardly secretive, are they?

Unlike Fred here. Why don't you tell us something about yourself, Fred?"

Frederick's face flushed under the spotlight of Edna's gaze.

"His name is Frederick," said Marjorie, leaping to his defence for some unknown reason. "And he doesn't have to tell us anything unless he wishes to do so."

"And now that's you told," Horace laughed.

Edna shrugged. "Suit yourself." She forked a boiled egg, elegantly dressed to look like a chicken, and stuffed it in her mouth. "I recognise that bad-tempered woman, but I can't remember where from."

"Which one?" asked Marjorie, although she could guess who Edna was referring to.

"The diva who made the theatrical exit."

"Where from?" Marjorie quizzed, for once finding herself interested in what Edna had to say.

Faith joined them at the tail end of the conversation. "Are you referring to Dolores Hagman?"

So much for no gossip, thought Marjorie.

"Yeah. I've seen her before. I never forget a face, but the name doesn't ring any bells."

"She used to be an opera singer." All heads swung towards Frederick, who still had the faraway look in his eyes.

And a former love, no doubt, thought Marjorie. Edna was too busy battling to recall her own memories to notice, which was perhaps as well, or he would have got a grilling.

"You're right. I saw her in *Tosca* at the Manchester Opera House for my Dennis's birthday. Can't say I'm a fan, but my late husband loved the opera. I was on the stage as well, you know, but I'm more of an entertainer. I do a great *Big Spender* cover..."

No doubt, Frederick had already heard all of this on the flight over, but Edna spent the next twenty minutes entertaining them with tales of her times working the stages in the north of England. Marjorie knew her to be more of a lounge singer rather than anyone famous, but she had to admit her cousin-in-law had a pleasant voice and many amusing stories to go with it. She really was a dichotomy. At times like these, Marjorie found her interesting and a pleasure to be with. If only she didn't crave being the centre of attention all the time. For now, Edna was in her element, holding court to four avid listeners.

"Did I hear you say you were on the stage?" A large, arty-looking man called over from the other table, his booming voice causing everyone in the room to stop speaking.

"Are you talking to me?" Edna yelled back. The loud voice was hardly necessary in the quiet that had ensued.

"Yes, I thought I heard you say you were on the stage. So was I. I did Shakespeare, what about you?" The man appeared to be in his sixties and wore a loud orange and blue cravat which he kept fiddling with.

"Oh, don't start that again," said the other man at the same table. Well-turned-out with neatly cut white hair, he was yawning for effect. "I beg you, madam, ignore him. He will bore you to tears with stories of his days travelling Europe acting in dull Shakespeare plays. I personally can't see what the fuss is about. I'm sure he was good in his day, but the man's been dead for centuries, and yet, people who don't have a clue what he wrote pretend to revere his work in order to make themselves sound intelligent."

Marjorie could see Edna had found a kindred spirit in this new man. Her cousin-in-law wasn't fond of Shakespeare, either.

Faith intervened before an argument started.

"Major Jeffries, let's leave each to their own, shall we?"

"I was a singer," Edna shouted to the first man over the muffled conversations that were starting up again.

"I see." The man sniffed loudly and lost interest, deciding at that point to leave his table. “I’m going for a walk. I’ll see you at dinner,” he said to his companions.

“Don’t mind him,” said the man Faith had called Major Jeffries. “He’s a pretentious prig.”

“Dad! Leave him alone. He’s tired, that’s all; you know he hates flying.” Turning to the others, the latest speaker introduced herself. “I’m Denise. This is my father, Simon. Percy Gainsborough is the one who just left, and this is his wife, Martha. She still works on the stage, don’t you, Martha?”

“More behind the stage than on it. Much to my husband’s disgust, I direct contemporary plays.”

“That must make for some interesting discussions,” Marjorie chuckled. “I’m Marjorie and this is my cousin-in-law, Edna Parkinton.”

“And your husbands, I presume?” said Major Jeffries.

“Goodness me, no, Major. This is Horace, Horace Tyler – Edna and I met him on a previous holiday – and this is Frederick Mackworth, who we just met today."

"Pleased to meet you all," said Horace politely.

"Frederick Mackworth, you say? I remember that name," said Martha. "Didn't you go out with my sister?"

Frederick flushed from the neck up. "If your sister is Dolores Plenrith, we walked out together many years ago. Of course, she wasn't Hagman back then."

"Haven't you heard? She's not married now, but she hasn't bothered changing the name." Major Jeffries chortled. "Her husband packed up and left with her young protégé. Perhaps you can cheer her up. A more bitter woman you won't meet."

"Simon!" said Martha. "You really should stop insulting people. It's not nice, and she is my sister after all."

"You can't kid me; you dislike her as much as I do, but I tell the truth. It's hardly my fault if people don't like it. Mind you, I bet she was a looker back then."

Frederick fiddled with his tie. "It was all a long time ago. We both moved on."

"I heard you married a doctor. Is she here?" asked Martha.

"My wife died five years ago." Frederick looked down at his hands.

Not liking the fact she was being left out, Edna unwittingly came to Frederick's rescue. "Interesting we all have connections to the stage, ain't it? Apart from Horace here, he's in avionics, and Marge never had to work in her life, her being a lady. And, she married well." There was that bitter tone again, the one Edna used when reminding Marjorie of her good fortune. Her late husband's father had inherited the family fortune while Edna's father had been cast out.

"I do enjoy the theatre, along with Shakespeare *and* the opera." Marjorie held Edna's gaze, not blinking. Why did this woman gall her so? The late Ralph Snellthorpe's uncle had been a gambling addict and a womaniser. Edna was well aware on her rational days that neither she nor her brother would have got a penny from her father, who would have squandered it all away. She also needed reminding every so often that her father had left her mother to fend for herself and the two children.

"*Lady* Marjorie, is it? Well, I'd better watch my Ps and Qs," said Major Jeffries.

"Where does your title come from, Major?" asked Edna, not willing to be nudged out of the conversation quite so easily.

"I was an army man, as were my father and grandfather before me. Grandfather fought in the Somme. One of the few who returned alive, but his nerves were shot to pieces, poor man. Still, he did his duty for king and country."

Marjorie reflected sadly that many people who had survived the Great War, as it was called, never spoke of it. Her father had been at Ypres for the battles there, but it was a taboo subject in their household, that particular war. Having seen enough documentaries exploring the horrors of both world wars, but WWI in particular, Marjorie wasn't surprised that most of the men wanted to leave it in the past. But she had no doubt they suffered flashbacks in the recesses of their minds.

Once the topics of Shakespeare and titles were dropped, Horace and the major became engrossed in a conversation about avionics. Martha paired with Edna, joining her for a drink in the bar, while Denise discussed the itinerary with Faith. Marjorie's attempts at bringing Frederick out of his doldrums failed miserably, so she gave up.

"I think I'll go and prepare for the evening," she said to no-one in particular.

Frederick took his cue. "Good idea. Time for me to do the same."

Faith was the only one to look up and wave. Edna called out as Marjorie passed her and Martha at the bar.

"Are you going to join us, Marge?"

"No, thank you. I'm going to unpack and get ready. If you like, I'll meet you down here at around five-thirty for a pre-dinner drink."

"Okay. See you then."

Frederick had disappeared by the time Marjorie arrived at the lift. She wondered what had happened between him and the woman named Dolores Hagman. There was certainly more to it than *walking out together,* as he'd so nicely put it. She would have thought Dolores a stage name rather than her real name, but Frederick had said she was previously Dolores Plenrith, so possibly it was her given name.

Whatever had gone on in the past, Frederick had looked as if he'd seen a ghost when he noticed Dolores storm out of the room. His reaction left Marjorie with the impression their breakup hadn't come from his side. The effect her appearance – or rather, disappearance – had already had on him would make for an interesting evening at the opera.

I wonder if she will be as affected by meeting a former love as he was. Somehow, Marjorie imagined not.

Chapter 3

"Did you say your cousin's titled?"

Martha and Edna had been making small talk at the bar when Marge passed by. As Martha sipped the white wine from her glass, Edna was having trouble making her out. She seemed friendly enough, but there was no light in the dreary ginger-brown eyes. She was plain to look at and didn't appear to be making much effort to glam herself up any. Edna was itching to pluck out the three long hairs protruding from a mole on the woman's chin.

Martha looked quizzically at Edna, who reluctantly forced herself to stop staring at the offending hairs and reply.

"Yeah, but don't hold that against her. Marge's all right underneath all that stiff and starchy persona. She can be a hoot when she wants to be."

"Oh. I wasn't sure the two of you got on," said Martha.

"She likes to pretend we don't, always telling people we're cousins-*in-law* rather than cousins, but we're a good match in many ways. Complete opposites, mind you. I get on her nerves sometimes 'cos I speak as I find – a bit like your Major Jeffries and your old man, from what I've seen."

"You're right. I think that's why Percy and Simon argue so much. They're too alike, although Simon's right about my husband. He can be a snob at times and he's far too loud, but he's harmless beneath the bark."

"Marge comes across as a snob to some people. When she goes over the top, I wind her up big time; otherwise, we're good friends." Edna wondered if the friendship was more on her own side than Marge's, but she liked to think it was mutual. "I saw your sister in an opera once, *Tosca*. My Dennis – he's dead now, God rest his soul – loved the opera."

Martha's lips twitched at the mention of her sister. "Dolores was a talented singer, but I'm afraid the booze and cigarettes have taken their toll on her voice. She's quite bitter about it, that and her messy divorce."

"Shame. Although I'm not a fan of the genre, she was good. Is she a bit of a diva?"

"What makes you say that?"

"Her unseemly departure, for one thing. I'm a gal who likes to make an entrance, but her ostentatious exit was quite spectacular. Certainly got her noticed."

"Oh, that. We're used to it, but yes, I suppose you could say she's a drama queen. She always has been. Dolores is older than me, but you wouldn't know it because of all the work she's had done."

"I've been down the Botox route myself, but I stopped. I didn't want to end up looking like a plasticine doll, not to mention the expense." Edna chortled. Martha smiled, but the dullness in her eyes remained.

"Dolores has never allowed lack of money to stand in the way of her spending. I'd be worried sick if I spent money like she does. Percy doesn't earn that much; to be honest, next to nothing these days. He's been getting fewer and fewer roles of late. We live comfortably enough, though, because I'm reasonably well paid, but I like to be careful."

"Do you like your work?" Edna asked, not feeling wholly comfortable discussing personal finance with a relative stranger. *Marge would say it was unseemly, but then she has money to burn, so doesn't need to talk about it.*

"My work is fun, but what I really want is to be a writer. I've written quite a few manuscripts and screenplays and would love to write and direct my own work." For the first time, a sparkle appeared in the other woman's eyes, but it disappeared quickly. "It's a cutthroat world out there. Very few scriptwriters get to see their work played out in the theatre." Martha took another sip of wine before speaking wistfully. "I thought I'd finally got a big break, but it turned out to be another shattered dream."

"Sorry to hear that," said Edna. *Boy, is this woman draining. Talk about woe is me. I wonder if that's how I sound in Marge's ears sometimes.* "Maybe your day will come. I always dreamed of being a famous singer, but I still got by singing in clubs. It was a good enough life. Now, I'm enjoying retirement. I'm hoping me and Marge will do a load more trips before I depart this earth." Edna decided to move the subject on. "Funny coincidence, your sister's boyfriend showing up, isn't it?"

"I don't remember ever meeting him, although his name was mentioned a lot back in the day. My parents said he and Dolores were close. I was still living at home in Norwich and had been ill for a while. Dolores had moved to Bath. I think that's where they met. She's never mentioned him to me, but my parents told me he married a doctor when I asked what had happened to them. Dolores doesn't talk about anything much other than herself. I think your diva description fits her well."

Edna laughed. Frederick had obviously cared about the diva. He'd been even more sullen during the buffet than when they'd met on the flight coming over.

"I reckon our Fred's a bit of a melancholic."

Martha's eyes shot up from her drink, darting around the place. Edna wondered if she'd missed something.

"Are you all right?"

"Yes. It's just I suffered from depression back then. I wonder if that's why I never met Mr Mackworth. Not that I would have, anyway. Dolores thought she was too good for our family most of the time. My parents indulged her." The bitter tone had returned.

"Is there a big age gap between the two of you?"

"Seven years. I'm about to turn sixty – one reason for this happy gathering."

Dolores looked older than sixty-seven, thought Edna, and Fred had to be late-seventies. She wondered if it had been the age gap that split the two lovers up all those years ago.

Martha continued in her doleful voice. “Although I’m surprised Dolores came, really. It’s not as if she enjoys my company, and she certainly doesn’t get on with Percy or the others. I expect it was because Chloe was coming.”

“Chloe’s her daughter?”

The twitching lips returned, then they tightened, but Martha didn’t get to answer as Horace rescued Edna.

“I’m just off to change for dinner. Will we be meeting for a drink beforehand?”

Edna took her opportunity. “Yes, Marge said we’d meet here at five-thirty. I’d better get upstairs myself and change into my glad rags, ready for our outing. I guess we’ll be seeing you later?” she said to Martha.

“I’m sure you will.”

“Right then,” Edna grabbed Horace’s arm and led him towards the lifts. “She’s an odd one,” she said when they were out of Martha’s earshot. “We seem to have loads in common in some ways. But I think she’s unhappy – from what little she told me, she’s had a tough life living in her sister’s shadow – yet I can’t take to her.”

“She seems pleasant enough to me, unlike her husband. I’d say he’s a tough man to live with; he’d be enough to make anyone miserable.”

“I won’t argue with you on that one. Once met, never forgotten. She says he thinks he’s superior, but he’s all right underneath it all. I’d rather live with a thorn bush myself.”

They both laughed, taking up where they had left off on the last holiday. Horace was fun.

Chapter 4

Faith explained the history of The National Opera, also known as The Romanian National Opera, on the bus journey from the hotel. It had apparently opened post World War I in 1919, with *Aida* being the first opera ever performed there. Marjorie was pleased that most of the party was listening to Faith's informative talk while the minibus driver negotiated the busy evening traffic. The Romanians' driving wasn't the worst Marjorie had experienced, but she certainly wouldn't consider it safe. Drivers seemed to overtake when they shouldn't, honking their horns if another vehicle dared to get in the way.

“There are a few things I must mention before we arrive,” said Faith. “First, there’s no bar inside, although there might be a table set up in the foyer where you can purchase drinks and snacks during the break. Because there’s no guarantee of that, we’ve brought a stock of mineral water. It will be hot inside, so please help yourself to a bottle as you leave the minibus. We’ve also got a supply of hand fans in case it gets too hot for you during the performance. There’s no air conditioning inside the building either, so let’s hope the night’s not too stuffy.”

Judging by the weather so far, Marjorie deduced it would almost certainly be stuffy inside a non-air-conditioned building.

“I would also suggest you don’t drink too much unless you really need to, as the toilet facilities are limited. The driver tells me they are usually clean, but probably not to UK standards.”

“I wish she’d said all this before we got on this bus,” groaned Edna. “I’d have stayed in the bar.”

Faith continued, “If you’re desperate to eat, there are a few shops outside where you can buy extra drinks and snacks.”

“I don’t think food will be the issue after that delicious dinner,” said Marjorie to Edna.

“Are there any other toilets nearby?” Major Jeffries piped up.

Faith put the question to the driver in broken Romanian, then replied, “The driver doesn’t think so.”

“You’ll be all right, Dad, don’t worry.” Denise tried to sound reassuring.

“That’s all very well for you to say, you don’t have my blasted prostate.”

“Really? Do we have to go into your plumbing problems again?” Percy was no doubt taking the opportunity to get his own back for the earlier put down in the conference room.

“Gentlemen, don’t fret. There are toilets available in the theatre, just not as many as we’re used to in a venue with a capacity of nine hundred people. The locals, I'm informed, tend not to use the facilities."

"She's not selling it at all well, is she?" Horace chuckled. "Don't worry, ladies, I've brought our supplies. I've been before." He winked, opening his jacket to reveal a bottle of Scotch in his inside breast pocket. "It's not allowed, but no-one takes any notice."

Edna grinned. "I hope you've got a urinal in your pocket as well."

"I'm afraid not. For that, you'll have to join the fray."

After breaking the bad news, Faith returned to the topic of the building's history, but the groaning and murmuring continued for a while. Marjorie recognised this wasn't a group of people used to less than a five-star service.

Dolores the diva, as Edna had nicknamed her, hadn't even glanced in Frederick's direction during dinner, despite Marjorie overhearing her sister, Martha, telling her he was there. She'd blanked him completely, but wasn't overly friendly with anyone else either. From what Marjorie had witnessed, she treated her browbeaten daughter despicably, constantly belittling her and complaining about everything she tried to do. Even now, she could see the woman telling her daughter off about something. None of the gang of six had impressed her so far and Marjorie hoped that once they were in Bucharest with the wider tour, they wouldn't have to see much of the unpleasant sextet at all.

Marjorie glanced across the small aisle to where Horace was listening intently to Faith's spiel. Either that, or he was making a good pretence of doing so. She wondered whether he had really been to the opera house before or was just trying to impress; she had learnt from their previous meeting not to take everything he said at face value. He liked to dazzle and was prone to exaggeration. That said, he was harmless and, during their last holiday, he had turned out to be a fun distraction for Edna, who had been grieving the loss of her husband and annoying Marjorie whenever she could.

Frederick stared sulkily out of the window. He looked dapper and not unattractive in his crisp black evening suit, sporting a neatly positioned black tie and another blue-and-white checked shirt which didn't quite match. Checked shirts appeared to be his thing. The poor man looked completely lost.

Edna nudged Marjorie from her musings. “They're off again,” she whispered.

Faith had stopped speaking as the driver parked up outside the opera house, giving their new companions the opportunity to resume their squabbling. *What a tiresome bunch they are,* thought Marjorie as the minibus came to a halt just outside the entrance.

“Perhaps we can avoid them once we're inside,” she said.

It was getting dark outside, but the baroque building they were about to enter was beautifully and subtly lit. Marjorie looked down from the top of the wide outside steps leading up to the entrance. They were packed with people climbing upwards.

"I'm glad they dropped us up here, Marge. You'd never have made it up them steps." Edna nudged her. "Especially when you never use your stick."

I'd like to use it on you sometimes, thought Marjorie. Instead, she said, "Watch your wig, it's flying at half-mast."

Edna's hands leapt to her wig, which was firmly in place. She laughed good-naturedly.

"You nearly had me there."

Marjorie smirked. *I did have you,* she thought, but was satisfied enough with the reaction not to rub it in.

Once they arrived inside the foyer, Marjorie stopped to look around, admiring the historic attempt at Rococo and Art Nouveau impressions. Crowds jostled past, showing their tickets to attendants who then allowed them to enter the grand theatre. Marjorie glanced over to where the toilets were and wondered if she should go before the show started. It appeared almost all of their party had the same idea and had left Faith waiting in the centre of the foyer with Denise Jeffries and the diva's daughter. The latter was probably pleased with the break.

"Come on, Marge, we'd better do the same before starting on Horace's Scotch."

"I have never drunk from a bottle in my life and I'm not about to start now," said Marjorie, following Edna towards the queue for the facilities.

"You're such a snob, Snellthorpe."

"And you're a slob, Edna Parkinton," retorted Marjorie, suppressing a giggle.

"I knew you'd be precious about that, so I lifted an extra water bottle. I'll empty it for you and Horace can pour some whisky into it."

"You're missing the point, Edna. It's still a bottle."

"But you'll drink water out of the bottle in your handbag," argued Edna.

"That's different. I have little choice in the matter."

An exasperated Edna huffed as she rushed into a free cubicle before an overzealous local pushed in. Marjorie would never be able to explain the difference between drinking water and whisky from a bottle, so why try?

Once they had all used the facilities, which had taken about thirty minutes, Faith called an usher who had been waiting for the group to come together. He escorted them through the main auditorium to the front row. Their seating was to the left of the stage, facing it. Apart from a bit of argy-bargy in the diva party about who would sit where, the process went without mishap. Horace and Frederick obligingly took the end two seats to Marjorie's left, with Edna sitting between Horace and Marjorie. Dolores's daughter sat on Marjorie's right, as Dolores had insisted she was seated more or less at the centre of the row. Major Jeffries was on Dolores's right next to the actor called Percy. Martha and Denise settled to their right with Faith taking the seat on the edge of the centre aisle. Faith walked along the row to make sure they had everything they needed.

"Can't you do anything about the heat?" Major Jeffries was already sweating under the bright lights, Marjorie noticed.

"I'm sorry, Major. As I said before, there's no air conditioning. I'll ask if we can open the doors until the show starts."

Faith returned a few minutes later with the usher who had shown them to their seats. He opened the side door, which Marjorie supposed was a secondary exit, and a draught of slightly cooler air headed their way.

"That's better. I thought I was going to have to remove me wig," said Edna loudly enough to draw a suppressed chuckle from the diva's daughter and a snort from Horace.

"Please don't," pleaded Marjorie. She never quite knew when Edna was teasing, but wouldn't put it past her to make an exhibition of herself. "It's such a lovely wig – do you know it takes years off you?" she added, hoping that would be enough to remove the thought from her companion's mind.

Edna's hands moved to pat the bleached-blonde number she had donned for the evening. Marjorie's cousin-in-law had a plentiful supply of wigs, which had confused Marjorie when they had become reacquainted during a river cruise from Amsterdam until Edna had revealed the sad reason behind the collection.

"Do you think so? The red one's still my favourite, but men like blondes," she chortled.

"Why should you care?" Marjorie whispered.

Horace chose that moment to offer Edna a swig of his Scotch, so Marjorie took the opportunity to look around the auditorium. The lights were bright white at present, which made it easy to see people coming in and filling up the floor seats. There were three rows of balconies with seating on both sides of the auditorium, the top ones housing fewer people than the other two. The closed stage curtains were faded, looked tatty and were in need of repair, not to mention a good wash. The more she looked, the more she realised the whole place needed refurbishment. It looked as though no money had been invested in recent years.

“This would have looked wonderful in its day.”

“I agree. It could do with an upgrade, but you can see beyond that to its history, can’t you?” The meek voice coming from the woman on Marjorie’s right surprised her.

“Did I say that out loud? Gosh, sometimes I believe I’m only thinking something and I’m clearly not! I agree with you, but it’s a shame to see it in this condition, isn’t it? I expect whoever built it would shudder if they saw the flaky paint.”

The woman smiled, a pleasant enough smile, but the green eyes were blank.

“I don’t think anyone formally introduced us. I’m Marjorie, Marjorie Snellthorpe.”

“Chloe, Chloe Hagman. This is my mother, Dolores.” Chloe turned to Dolores. “Mum, this is Marjorie.”

Dolores acknowledged Marjorie with a nod, her upturned nose making her look even more the diva. *Stop it, Snellthorpe. You're sounding like Edna.* Her hand went to her mouth to check she hadn't said that out loud.

"Lady Snellthorpe, isn't it? Simon mentioned there was a titled lady among us." Dolores sounded indifferent and Marjorie didn't like her tone.

"I rarely use the title. People call me Marjorie."

"In that case, you can call me Lolita. Dolores means sorrow or suffering, you know, and how have I suffered, but now I intend to go by the name Lolita and act like it."

"Mother!" Chloe sounded shocked. "Someone might think you're serious."

"I'm sure Lady Marjorie knows what it means."

Marjorie did indeed know the meaning of the name Lolita: precocious or seductive. Although Dolores was sometimes shortened to Lolita, among other things, she was grateful she didn't have to respond. The lights dimmed and an announcement in Romanian was greeted with loud applause as the curtains squeaked open.

"Let the show commence," whispered Edna in Marjorie's left ear, her breath smelling of whisky. Marjorie felt that somehow the show had already begun, and it wasn't the one about to be played out on the stage.

Chapter 5

Towards the end of the first act, Dolores's incessant humming, which had started quietly, was becoming uncontrollable. Marjorie feared she might deliver her own rendition of an aria at any moment, as she appeared to be more and more drawn into the performance. People in the row behind were tutting and shushing, but Dolores ignored them and continued, oblivious as the scene built to a crescendo.

"Shut up, woman." Marjorie heard Major Jeffries's firm voice cut through the increasingly hysterical humming. His rebuke did the trick, jolting the woman out of her trancelike state.

The first act closed to rapturous applause. The company had put on an impressive performance, although it would have sounded so much better if the equipment and speakers had been more modern and positioned all around the auditorium rather than just at the front.

“Bravo, bravo,” shouted Percy, standing. Horace soon followed this with an ovation of his own.

Once the clapping had stopped, a stampede of people hurried towards the exits, either to use the facilities or possibly to make a dash for the shops outside for sustenance.

“We’re going to stretch our legs, are you coming?” Edna prodded Marjorie.

“I think I’ll stay here for a while. You go.”

Edna and Horace left through the lower exit, but came back a few minutes later.

“Painters in the way. They won’t let us through,” Horace explained before they headed up the stairs towards the main foyer.

Marjorie remained seated, not inclined just yet to battle her way through the crowds. If need be, she would make her exit towards the end of the intermission. Everyone had vacated their part of the front row except for Frederick, who remained on the end seat, numbly staring straight ahead.

“Did you enjoy the performance?” Marjorie asked, making him jump for the second time that day.

“Sorry? Yes, it was tremendous considering what they don’t have.”

“You mean in terms of modern equipment?”

“Yes. Mind you, it probably made it sound more like it would have done when the place first opened.” Frederick half-grinned. He was clearly an opera fan. Marjorie was certain there was an interesting man beneath his bashfulness. That, and the effect that Dolores Hagman had left on him.

“Did you try any of Horace’s Scotch?” she asked, steering the conversation away from anything too personal.

“To be honest, I brought a bottle of brandy with me. Would you like some? I could ask that usher fellow to find you a glass.”

“If it’s not too much trouble, I’d love to join you in a toast.”

“I’ll be back in a jiffy.”

Frederick was gone, leaving Marjorie fighting the urge to use the facilities; a battle she would have won in her younger days, but not now. Reluctantly, she left her seat and climbed the steps.

About half of the audience members had returned to their seats. It was nice to see a lot of families with children. She wondered if there were any private facilities upstairs for the people on the balconies, but wasn’t prepared to make what might be a wasted journey without assurance.

Once she arrived in the foyer, she was pleasantly surprised. It appeared many of the locals had indeed gone outside. Perhaps they knew of other facilities. Judging by the smoke, however, she was certain their departure was for other reasons; there was a strict no-smoking policy in the theatre. Faith had also told them there was a strict no-alcohol policy, so she hoped Frederick wasn't disclosing to the usher what the glass was for.

There was a small queue outside the ladies, which moved swiftly. Marjorie was back in the foyer in time to hear, though not understand, the announcements that she presumed told them the second half was about to begin. When she got back to her seat, she noticed a vacant space where Dolores had been sitting, and raised an eyebrow at Chloe, who gave her a wide smile. Just as the curtain opened and all the doors closed, Frederick reappeared out of puff. He flopped down in the seat on the other side of Horace, not looking her way. He had either forgotten about her brandy, or hadn't been able to find a glass.

The second-half performance was more pleasant without the humming racket that had accompanied the first, but Marjorie was puzzled as to where Dolores could be. She hadn't been in the toilets and Marjorie hadn't seen her in the foyer. Perhaps she'd got fed up or had another argument and taken a taxi back to the hotel, although that would be strange considering how moved she had appeared by the first-half performance. Marjorie resisted the temptation to ask Chloe, who seemed so much happier without her mother. It wasn't the *done* thing to speak during an opera and she wouldn't risk the ire of the people in the row behind. Perhaps Dolores had been too late returning and wasn't allowed back inside.

With the final curtain calls and applause over, Marjorie turned to Chloe. "What happened to your mother? I do hope she's not ill."

Chloe looked around as if suddenly realising for the first time that her mother hadn't come back. Her hand went to her mouth and her eyes widened.

"Sugar! I'm going to be in for it now. She said she was going for a smoke outside while I went to the ladies. She was nowhere to be seen when I got back, but I assumed she'd turn up. Then I forgot all about her. I've got a head like a sieve sometimes. She's always telling me that. I bet she was late and they refused to let her in once the show started. I'll get the blame now for not letting her know."

"I don't see why your mother would blame you. The announcements were loud enough to wake the dead when I was in the foyer. It might be wise for you to check she's all right, though."

"She'll have flown into a temper and got a taxi back to the hotel if they didn't let her in. I'd rather not ruin my evening just yet. I'll face her wrath when we get back."

Although Chloe was most probably right, Marjorie wouldn't be satisfied until they had checked on the annoying woman. As Chloe stood to chat with Denise Jeffries and her father, Marjorie decided she would ask Faith, who was making her way along the row, if she knew where the Hagman diva was.

"Did you enjoy the show?" Faith asked.

"I did, very much, thank you. But I'm concerned Dolores Hagman didn't return. She seemed to enjoy the first act far more than any of us. It doesn't make sense for her to miss the second half."

"What's that, Marge?" Edna asked.

"Dolores is missing."

"What do you mean, missing?" said Horace. "Just because the silly woman didn't come back in for the second half doesn't mean she's missing."

"What does Chloe say?" Faith asked.

"She told me the last time she saw her mother, Dolores was going outside for a cigarette. She doesn't seem at all worried and believes she may have returned to the hotel after being too late to get back in."

"A plausible explanation, one has to agree," said Horace, whose cheeks were flushed from either the heat or the Scotch.

"What's happening?" Frederick seemed to come out from under his spell and joined the four of them.

Horace explained the situation. “From what I’ve seen of the demanding woman, she’ll be attention seeking.”

“Don’t say that,” said Frederick.

Faith called Chloe over. “Chloe, would you mind phoning your mother and checking whether she’s at the hotel? I can’t leave with a guest unaccounted for.”

“She’ll have turned her phone off like the rest of us, but I’ll try.” Chloe dialled a number and handed her phone to Faith. “You talk to her if she answers; she’ll be too cross to tell me anything.”

Faith waited for what seemed like an age until someone answered the phone. “I’m sorry. Pardon? Slow down. I’m sorry, I don’t speak much Romanian... Just a minute... Are any of you fluent in Romanian?”

Horace held his hand out. “Give it to me.” He spoke into the phone. “*Da... da...*” Horace moved away from them, covering one of his ears to hear what was being said. Marjorie heard the word *politie* and knew something was amiss. She and the rest of the group crowded around Horace.

“We need to go outside immediately.” He looked at Chloe with sympathy. “I’m so sorry. It appears your mother may have had a heart attack. An ambulance is on the way, but the fellow I spoke to says she’s ice cold. I’ve asked him to call the police as well, just in case.”

Chloe swooned, but Percy Gainsborough caught her before she hit the floor and helped her into a seat. Everyone started speaking at once with Dolores’s companions gathering around Chloe, who was given water to drink.

“That lot will be useless. We’d better get outside and find out what’s going on,” said Edna. For once, Marjorie agreed she was right. Horace led the way and she, Edna, Frederick and Faith followed. They found Romanian paramedics and the police outside, attending to Dolores Hagman, who was sitting upright against the wall of the opera house.

The perfect place for an opera diva to breathe her last, thought Marjorie.

Chapter 6

Once the hullabaloo had died down, Marjorie found a moment to quiz a Romanian woman who thankfully spoke English. She was with the man who had conveyed the bad news to Horace via Dolores Hagman's phone and explained that while people were exiting the building, a young boy heard a phone with the same ringtone as his. He knew it wasn't his, because he had switched it to silent during the performance in accordance with the rules. The boy saw an elderly woman – Dolores – sitting against the wall, staring into space. Her phone was ringing and flashing in her lap.

The boy realised there was something wrong with the woman when he tried to tell her the phone was ringing. He reached for the phone automatically, but when he saw she was motionless, he became upset and handed the phone to the man who'd spoken with Horace. Then the boy's parents pulled him away. The woman Marjorie was speaking to had called for an ambulance while her companion explained to the man – Horace – on the other end of the phone that they had found the owner of the mobile and she was dead.

Marjorie thanked the woman for the information. She and Edna then observed a lot of gesticulating and excitable discussion before the police apparently agreed to release the body to the ambulance crew. They were told, via Horace, that the ambulance would take the body to the hospital morgue as first impressions were that Dolores had suffered a heart attack. There was no suggestion of foul play.

Chloe witnessed none of this activity as she was still inside the opera house. Edna went back inside, and emerged after a few minutes to tell Marjorie and Horace that Chloe was being half persuaded and half prised away from her seat to join them.

By the time Chloe arrived outside, the ambulance crew had already loaded her mother into their vehicle. Faith encouraged Marjorie and the rest of the tour group to get back on board the minibus to return to the hotel. With Horace's help, Faith gave the police a list of people in the party and let them know they were staying at the Platinia.

The journey back to the hotel didn't take long, which was just as well as it passed in eerie silence. It was only when they arrived back in the hotel's warmth that the Hagman party started to talk among themselves. Martha, Dolores's sister and Chloe's aunt, took charge of the shocked woman, corralling her into the lift. Her husband, Percy, and the major's daughter, Denise Jeffries, helped. The major left them to it, saying he was going to grab a nightcap.

Faith appeared visibly shocked and stressed. She excused herself, saying she would need to file a report to the holiday firm and make some calls.

“Ladies, spending time with you two is never dull,” Horace chuckled. “Last time it was a tumble down the stairs and now it’s a heart attack.”

“Let’s hope that’s all it was,” said Marjorie.

“Here she goes again. Somebody dies, it must be murder,” said Edna, scornfully.

“What do you mean, murder?” Frederick had barely said a word since the sad discovery. Now his face had taken on a dark shade of raspberry.

I wonder if he has high blood pressure, thought Marjorie. *And I’d like to know where my glass of brandy got to.*

“Ignore my cousin, Fred.” Edna glared at Marjorie. “You remember we told you the last time we were together, a woman fell down the stairs? Well, she didn’t actually fall; she was pushed and the death was made to look like an accident. Now Marjorie believes every time someone dies, it must be foul play. She fancies herself as a regular Miss Marple."

"But, according to you," Frederick looked at Horace in earnest, "the police and the paramedics said she died of a heart attack."

"They did, and it seems highly likely they are correct in their assumption," Horace confirmed. "Sorry, Marjorie, I can't see any murder here."

"I'm sure you, and they, are right," said Marjorie. "It just pays to be thorough before jumping to conclusions, that's all. Why don't we join the major for a drink. I'd love a *brandy.*" She couldn't resist the veiled barb, but it fell on deaf ears. Frederick had returned to his own little world.

"What a good idea," said Horace. "You sit down and I'll get the drinks. I know what Edna likes. What are you having, Fred?"

"It's Frederick, not Fred. I'll come with you."

The two men headed to the bar, Horace with a spring in his step and Frederick with shoulders slumped woefully. Marjorie and Edna approached the major's table.

"Do you mind if we join you?" Marjorie asked, which was a somewhat redundant question as the major didn't get to answer before Edna plonked herself down in a chair.

"Blimey! What a night," she said, blowing air from puffed cheeks. "I wish I'd stayed behind. I could hardly breathe in that theatre, it was so bloomin' hot, and to top it off, we've got a death on our hands."

"Oh, but what an ending!" said the major. "Dolores always knew how to make an entrance, but her exit was even more spectacular. If she wasn't actually dead, I'd say it was staged."

"Did you know her well?" Marjorie asked as the other two men returned from the bar with a tray of drinks and sat down.

"I know, or rather knew, her ex-husband better, but he did the dirty on her and the others, my daughter included, won't forgive him. Percy, her brother-in-law, is a lifelong friend. We argue all the time, but underneath the spats, we get on well. If I'm honest, I knew as much of Dolores as I wanted to. I don't take to these temperamental types who think they're better than anyone else."

He turned to Frederick. "Sorry if that upsets you. I heard you had a fling with Dolores once, but I say it as it is, and if people don't like it—" The major raised his glass in the air.

"It wasn't a fling. We were engaged to be married," Frederick snapped.

"You didn't say," said Marjorie.

"Well, I'm saying now." Frederick's face darkened.

"Hey, don't take it out on us if you've got poor taste in women," Edna growled.

"What happened?" asked Marjorie.

Frederick took a gulp of brandy before answering, avoiding eye contact with any of them. "The lead up to the wedding was perfect.

We decked the church out as it should be. Dolores had just finished a tour. She walked up the aisle to meet me at the altar. She looked stunning. I wasn't good looking, but I wasn't bad either. I felt like the luckiest man on earth when she got to the front of the church. Then, just like one of the operatic tragedies she starred in, Dolores lifted the veil from her face, looked me in the eye with a cold, hard stare, shook her head, turned and walked back the way she'd come. The bridesmaids had no idea what to do with themselves, so they ran after her."

As if they were a bunch of goldfish in a tank, everyone's mouths dropped open.

"Why would she do such a thing on your wedding day?" Marjorie asked.

"I don't know. She never said. For years, I've asked myself that same question. My friends said it was the age gap – she was twelve years younger than me – but I don't think that was the reason. I felt like a reject. I wanted to ask her tonight, but couldn't find the courage. You know, she didn't even look at me once since I got here." Frederick gulped back the rest of his brandy.

Major Jeffries put a hand on his shoulder. "You have my sympathy, man. Must have been an awful thing to get over. But she got her comeuppance, as it were. Her husband, my old pal, took his new lover – her protégé – to see her last performance. Sat in the front row, exhibiting his bit of stuff, and from what I hear, walked out halfway through her aria."

"Did she know he was having an affair?" Edna asked.

"Apparently not, but she did that night." Major Jeffries grinned.

"Sounds like they deserved each other," Horace said. "Still, let's not be malicious. We should show a bit of respect, eh? The woman's hardly cold. Best to think positively about her."

Marjorie looked at Frederick, who appeared to be relaxing. Was it due to the news that someone had publicly humiliated the fiancée who'd jilted him at the altar, or was it the effects of the alcohol?

"Do you think you'll continue with the holiday, Major?" asked Horace.

"Call me Simon. I'm not in the army now. From my perspective, I don't see why not. It'll depend on Percy and Martha, of course. Denise will want to do what they do, but I suspect Chloe might want to go home. Her mother treated her abominably, but blood is blood, I suppose."

At that moment, Faith joined them, looking dishevelled, which was a rarity from what Marjorie remembered of her.

"How are you all? I'm so sorry about the shock."

"We can hardly hold you responsible for someone's health emergency," said Marjorie, reassuringly.

"That's true. Horrible thing to happen on the first night, though. I've just been to see Miss Hagman. Her aunt's with her, and they are both determined to continue with the trip."

"Well, that answers your question, Horace," said Simon Jeffries. "It looks like we will not be going home. I must say, I'm pleased. I've been looking forward to seeing Bucharest before cruising the Danube and visiting all those places on the way to Budapest."

"What will happen to the diva?" asked Edna in her usual blunt manner.

Faith scrunched her forehead momentarily. "Oh, you mean Mrs Hagman. Her daughter has given me the insurance details. I'll contact the company to arrange repatriation as soon as the Romanian police say it's okay to move her."

"Will there be a post-mortem?" Marjorie enquired.

"The police and paramedics didn't feel one was necessary, but it will be up to the Romanian equivalent of a pathologist and the medics. It was a sudden death after all, so I would have thought it warrants one, although Chloe says she'd rather her mother was just sent back to England. Once we get the go ahead, either

Martha Gainsborough or Chloe will contact the UK undertakers."

"Well, that's that, then. I think I'll go to bed," said Major Jeffries. Marjorie was struggling to think of him as anything other than the major; it suited him much better than Simon.

"Just one thing," said Faith. "Considering this evening's events, we'll be leaving at eleven in the morning rather than ten to give the family a little more time to gather their thoughts and, if the police allow, sort out Mrs Hagman's belongings. We'll still have plenty of time to board our flight."

"Fine by me," said the major. "Goodnight all. See you at breakfast no doubt, unless another one of us kicks the bucket in the night." They could hear his guffaw all the way through the lobby.

"I'm going up too. I've had quite enough excitement for one night," said Horace.

Faith left Marjorie, Edna, and Frederick to finish their drinks. Frederick had refilled his glass from his personal supply.

“Did you ever find that usher you were looking for during the break?” asked Marjorie. “I couldn’t help noticing you only just made it back in time for the second half.”

Frederick flinched. “I got lost in the crowds, then realised I needed the gents. The major was coming indoors while I was in the queue. I’m not sure if he smokes or went out for a breath of fresh air. Anyway, by the time I got out again, they were about to close the doors. An usher let me through, muttering in Romanian. You’re right, I made it just as the show was about to start.”

“Let me get this right. You saw Major Jeffries coming in from outside? He didn’t mention seeing Dolores,” said Marjorie, frowning.

“Perhaps that’s because he didn’t see her,” said Edna. “There were crowds of people hanging around outside, probably trying to cool off. Me and Horace debated whether to go out ourselves, but the queue to the ladies was massive by then. The major and the diva were hardly best buddies, were they, Marge? If he had seen her, I'm sure he would have avoided her like the plague."

"It's just odd he didn't mention it, that's all. As Frederick says, perhaps he was sneaking out for a cigarette. I doubt his daughter would approve. She appears to henpeck her father, if you ask me. Anyway, I think it's time for me to retire for the night. I'll see you in the morning."

"I'll come up with you. We can't have you falling over when you insist on not using your stick." Edna drained her glass and joined her.

Marjorie tutted. "As you wish, but I'm quite all right without it, thank you."

Edna took a left when they exited the lift, and Marjorie was thankful to turn right. There was a lot to mull over. It was going to be another one of those sleepless nights.

Chapter 7

Following a subdued breakfast the next morning, Marjorie, Edna and Horace split up and returned to their rooms to pack. They had agreed to meet in the coffee lounge as soon as they were ready.

Marjorie's suitcase and hand luggage were all ready to go; knowing they were only staying here for the one night, she had barely unpacked anything. On the way to meet the others, she noticed Faith in the lobby, speaking with a uniformed police officer and a plain clothes-detective. The trio appeared to be having an earnest whispered conversation. The man and woman departed and Faith headed her way.

“From where I’m standing, that didn’t look like good news,” Marjorie remarked.

Faith’s frown deepened. “I’m afraid there’s been a complication. I need to gather everyone together. We’ll meet in the conference room where we had lunch yesterday in fifteen minutes. Would you let Edna and your other two friends know?”

“Of course,” said Marjorie. “I take it the police now suspect foul play?”

“Sort of. I’ll explain everything when we meet. I’d better track down the others. Did you see any of them at breakfast?”

Marjorie rolled her eyes, remembering the fractious tittle-tattling between Percy and the major. “I believe the men returned to their rooms. The ladies, I was told, had a room service breakfast.”

“Thank you. I’ll see you shortly.”

Marjorie hesitated before approaching Frederick, who had already brought his suitcase downstairs and was sitting in the coffee lounge reading a newspaper. He hadn't joined them for breakfast, but he appeared, at least from the outside, to be more in control than he had since his shock encounter – if they could call it that – with his almost-bride the day before.

"Faith has asked me to let you know she needs to speak to us in the conference room where we lunched yesterday."

Frederick looked up from his paper. "Why?"

"She didn't say. I'm just going in search of Edna and Horace. They said they would join me in here."

No sooner had the words come out of her mouth than she heard raucous laughter on the other side of the room. *It appears I've found them*, she thought. Edna and Horace, with the addition of Denise Jeffries, appeared to be in good humour.

"Excuse me," Marjorie said.

"Hello, Marge. Where did you get to? Denise has just been entertaining us with stories of

Percy's antics. Seems he was quite the joker in his day. He and the major go way back."

"Yes, the major said that last night, didn't he?" *Does Edna never listen?* She nodded politely to Denise. "I'm sorry to interrupt, but Faith would like us to join her in the Picasso Conference Room. It appears there's been a development."

"Regarding the late Dolores Hagman, I presume?" Horace was quick off the mark. "Funny business, that."

"Last night, you said it was only to be expected at our age," moaned Edna. "You need to make up your mind.

"From what Frederick revealed last night, she was much younger than him, and, by implication, us," said Marjorie.

"Yeah, Martha told me she was seven years older than her which puts her at sixty-seven, but she didn't wear well did she? Despite all the Botox. Anyway, Marge, what is this *development*, as you put it?"

"We'll find out shortly, I don't doubt," Marjorie answered.

The three of them polished off their coffees and stood, ready to go.

"I'd better let Dad know," said Denise.

"No need. When I saw Faith, she was on her way to contact the rest of your party. I'm sure they will be waiting for us." Denise looked angry, but Marjorie couldn't make out why as they made their way to the conference room.

Marjorie was right: the rest of the Hagman party were clamouring impatiently in the conference room, waiting to hear what Faith had to say.

"About time too!" exclaimed Percy when they entered. Frederick was already seated at the large conference table. Faith encouraged them to do the same.

Poor woman looks even more stressed than she did last night; this can't be good, thought Marjorie.

“Thank you all for coming at such short notice,” Faith began when everyone quietened down. “I’m afraid I’ve got some bad news. We’re going to have to stay in Cluj-Napoca for an extra day or two. The police aren’t satisfied Mrs Hagman died from natural causes and have requested a post-mortem.” Faith cast a glance towards Chloe. “I believe they contacted you about it earlier this morning?”

Chloe lowered her eyes, “Yes, but—”

“They can’t do that! I’ve paid for a holiday and I’m going to have one.” Percy Gainsborough slammed his hand hard onto the table for effect.

“I’m afraid you’ll find, dear fellow, they can do whatever they like,” said Major Jeffries philosophically.

“Well, I for one would like to stay if there’s any suggestion someone attacked my sister while she was outside.” Martha glared at her husband. “Show some respect, Percy.”

Percy ran a hand through his curly grey hair, but said no more. Marjorie had no problem imagining him as the villainous Claudius in *Hamlet* if he had ever been cast in the role.

“May I ask why the change of heart?” she quizzed, not wanting war to break out before they had received the facts. “And do the police, as Mrs Gainsborough suggests, suspect a random attack? Mrs Hagman didn’t look as if anyone had attacked her.”

“All I’ve been told is that fresh evidence has come to light which leads them to suspect Mrs Hagman might have been concerned for her life.”

“She said nothing to me,” said Chloe, wiping a tear from her eye and mascara along with it.

“Nor me,” said Martha.

“What fresh evidence and where from?” Major Jeffries demanded.

“The police inspector who came to visit me this morning told me they received a telephone call from someone in England.” Faith looked at Chloe. “I don’t know exactly what was said or who it was from, but it was enough to prompt them into investigating further."

"I bet it's that blasted Philippa stirring things up again. She can't keep her nose out of anything. I suppose you called her last night?" Percy glared accusingly at Chloe.

"No, she didn't," said Martha, patting the other woman's hand. "I did. Philippa had a right to know."

"What right? The woman's not even family," Percy snapped.

"She is, or was, to Dolores. They've been friends for around forty years." Martha rubbed her forehead. "Philippa mentioned nothing to me about calling the police, though. She was shocked, of course, but—"

"So we can thank you for our prolonged stay in Cluj-Napoca," snapped Major Jeffries, clearly no longer feeling so philosophical.

Faith intervened. "If the post-mortem, which is being carried out this afternoon, confirms Mrs Hagman died of a heart attack and there are no abnormal findings, we may leave tomorrow morning. Although, how I'll find flights at such short notice, I don't know. If they find anything else, the inspector said he would want to interview all of us, tonight or tomorrow."

"Damn and blast," said Percy. "Why couldn't you call the wretched woman after we got home?"

"Because she had a right to know, Percy," repeated Martha, tight lips twitching slightly. "Although, if I'd thought for one moment she was going to call the police, I might have waited. But, if Dolores didn't die from natural causes, it changes everything."

"And now, thanks to the wonderful Philippa..." unlike the major, Percy didn't go so far as to blame his wife, "...inventing some cock-and-bull story, we're all stuck here under suspicion."

"It's not all bad," said Denise. "I'll be happy to spend an extra day here. I could visit the art museums and take a stroll around the town."

"Not on your own, you won't, and I'm not going with you. Blasted hip's playing up." The major rubbed his right hip for effect. “Those seats were so damned uncomfortable last night. We ought to complain and get our money back.”

“You never stop complaining,” said Percy. “If it’s not you plumbing, it’s your hip.”

“Someone who has a gold medal in the complaints department won’t lecture me on the subject,” the major snapped, continuing to rub his hip.

“For once, I agree with your father, though, Denise,” continued Percy, ignoring the major. “You shouldn’t wander around a strange city on your own and I’m not going outside.”

“I’ll come with you,” said Chloe. “I could do with getting out. I don’t want to stay here and listen to constant arguing.”

Percy raised his eyebrows. “Oh look! The mouse has found her voice.”

“Leave her alone, Percy, I’m warning you. She’s just lost her mother.” Martha glared at her husband once more.

"Oh, all right," he shrugged. "Sorry, Chloe, I didn't mean any harm." Not waiting for a response, he looked at Faith. "I take it we're not under house arrest or anything and can leave the hotel?"

"You are free to do as you please. We won't hear anything more until later today, maybe not until this evening. I've arranged for our rooms to remain on an open booking. We have a few days' leeway before the river cruise starts; you just won't get to see as much of Bucharest as you were expecting if we're delayed beyond tomorrow."

"Let's hope it's all sorted out by this evening, then," Major Jeffries said. "I need to find a pharmacy, if they have such things in this city. I forgot my painkillers."

"Of course they have pharmacies, Dad. We're not in the back of beyond; we're still in Europe. I thought you said you didn't want to go out."

"Needs must, dear. A quick stroll to a pharmacy differs greatly from spending hours in art galleries. I know what you're like. And, as for this city, judging by the state of that theatre last night, we're very much in the back of beyond."

"I rather enjoyed the experience," said Marjorie. "Granted, the interior needed refurbishment, but the show was as good as any I've seen."

The major didn't appear convinced, but didn't argue.

"I know where there's a pharmacy," said Horace. "I used to stay here on business from time to time. I'll give you directions."

"I'd appreciate it."

"Don't get lost, Dad," said Denise, to which the major muttered something about being glad of the space and not going senile yet.

"I'd better contact head office and give them an update on what's happening," said Faith.

The company gradually dispersed, leaving Marjorie with Edna and Frederick.

"Looks like you might have been right after all, Marge. What say we do a little investigating of our own?"

Marjorie cast a sympathetic glance towards Frederick. "I'm so sorry."

"So am I," he said. "It's not that I felt anything for the woman anymore; it's just I wanted to ask her why she did what she did when everything appeared so perfect."

"Oh, you're not sorry she's dead, then?" Edna narrowed her eyes. "Just that you didn't get her to mend your wounds."

"Ignore her. She doesn't mean half of what she says. Did Dolores really never give you any clues as to why she walked out on you?"

He shook his head. "None. She was always headstrong and loved a drama, but I never imagined for one moment she would play one out at our wedding."

"You must have hated her," said Edna, not so easily put off and never one to hesitate with her opinions.

"Hate is such a strong word. I was angry and confused, even heartbroken, but I don't believe I ever hated her."

"Still, love spurned. That's a powerful motive for murder," said Edna.

"Edna! As Frederick has already explained, their relationship and what happened occurred decades ago."

"I doubt that will count for much if someone knocked her off. I've heard Romanian jails can be very unpleasant. He's bound to be the prime suspect."

Frederick didn't appear angry at Edna's outburst. He just smiled.

"If you knew me at all, you would know how ludicrous that sounds. I'm a pacifist. If there had been a war in my younger years, I would have been a conscientious objector. That's the only way I would ever have ended up in any prison."

"Even if I believe you," said Edna, "you must realise how it looks. Ex-lover shows up after all these years. All that buried trauma and hurt boils over in a moment of madness."

A glimmer of fear crossed Frederick's eyes. "Surely no-one would seriously believe I killed her?"

"We're forgetting one thing," said Marjorie, who herself had come up with a mental theory similar to Edna's. "The cause of death could still be a heart attack. Besides, if this was murder, it was most likely premeditated. Without a telephone call from this old friend, if that's who made it, none of us would be any the wiser."

"That's where we should start, then. We need to find out if it was this Philippa person who called, and if so, what she told the police. Then at least we'll know exactly what they do."

"How do you suggest we find that out?" asked Frederick.

"We call Philippa," said Marjorie, reading her cousin-in-law's mind. "We'll find out who she is from Percy Gainsborough. He obviously dislikes the woman, but if his wife has her contact details, it's likely he does too, or at least knows how to get them."

"What makes you think he'll tell us anything?" Frederick asked.

"It's us now, is it?" Edna laughed.

"Well, if you're right and I'm going to be chief suspect, I'd like to get on the front foot, as it were."

"He'll tell us what we want to know because he's a bitter sort of man," said Marjorie. "His type always speaks up. If I'm right, he'll be dying to tell someone his theories, and I doubt his wife or the major would listen. All we need to do is catch him without Martha and get him to tell us about Dolores Hagman's long-time friend. We can begin by asking why she would want to stir up trouble for them, and it won't be long before he's spilling his vitriol. Give him a little sympathy and we'll have her name, history and, if we're lucky, telephone number in no time."

"I'm realising you're a canny sleuth, Lady Marjorie."

"Less of the Lady, please."

"And me," piped up Edna. "Remember last time, Marge, it was me who helped you solve that crime."

"You and Horace, if I have to concede to such a notion. I believe I solved the crime and you happened upon me at the right time."

Before Edna could say anything to the contrary, Horace reappeared.

"I take it you've been hatching up a plan of action. We can't leave this to the police; we could be here for months. Either that, or they'll arrest the wrong man."

"What makes you think the killer – if there is one – is a man?" asked Marjorie.

"Call me old-fashioned, but I don't like to think of the fairer sex committing murder."

Edna snorted. "Old fashioned? You're a dinosaur, Horace Tyler. I don't know how you've got so far in business with that attitude."

Horace grinned. “You forget, I own the business. I delegate. Besides, I’m not such an old fossil that I don’t know when to keep shtum, which is more than I can say for someone around here.” He winked at Edna.

“Time to get on,” said Marjorie, fearing it was highly likely they would hear bad news later that day and wanting to be ahead in terms of information.

Chapter 8

Percy Gainsborough was heading out of the hotel when they got to the lobby.

"So much for him not wanting to go out," said Edna.

"We could follow him," suggested Horace.

Marjorie thought for a moment. They couldn't be described as fit and agile, and were all most likely, fifteen to twenty years older than Percy.

"I think we would be better waiting in the lobby until he returns and catch him on his way back."

“He might be younger than we are, but he’s overweight with high blood pressure,” Frederick said, as if reading her mind. “He won’t have got far.”

“How do you know that... about the high blood pressure, I mean?” Marjorie quizzed.

“I heard his wife reminding him to take his blood pressure pills earlier.”

“Come on,” said Frederick assertively. “We have to find out what we can about this Philippa woman. He might be out all day.”

“Did you never meet her when you and Dolores were together?”

“Never. What did Martha say – they’ve been friends for forty years? They must have met around the time the wretched woman humiliated me in church.”

Frederick sounded more scathing than hurt when he referred to Dolores’s unkind departure from his life. He seemed to have gained a new lease of life and was clearly not to be dissuaded, so they followed him into the busy street outside of the hotel.

It appeared their newfound detective was correct in his assumption. Percy hadn't got very far along the road. He was walking slowly, although Marjorie felt it was more to do with his deciding to take a stroll rather than his size or blood pressure. He was easily recognisable, wearing a garish patchwork shirt, a red boater and the same bright orange cravat he'd had on when they'd first met.

"Look natural, people," instructed Horace. "We're just out for a walk, remember that."

Edna, who up until then had been unusually quiet, probably trying not to sound breathless, straightened the bobbed black wig of the day. Her wig arranging was a habit which seemingly gave Edna confidence and prepared her for what might lie ahead; in this instance, a rebuke.

"Talk about stating the bloomin' obvious, Horace."

Marjorie noticed how Edna always used Horace's full name and found herself wondering whether there was a diminutive. She felt certain that if there were one, Edna would have found it, determined as the woman was never to call anyone by their given name.

Right on cue, Edna called back, “Come on, Marge, keep up. Why don’t you use your stick?”

“I’m quite all right. I’m doing as Horace suggested and behaving naturally. Unlike some.”

Edna was tearing along the path like a bulldozer, drawing attention to herself despite admonishing Horace a minute earlier for warning against that very thing. She ignored Marjorie’s comment and stormed ahead. Horace kept pace with her while Frederick walked alongside Marjorie.

“There’s an awful lot of traffic on this road, isn’t there?” he remarked.

“And people,” said Marjorie. “Do we still have our target in sight?” She was smaller than the rest of the group and could no longer see Percy because of a family taking up the whole pavement just in front of them. It was a glorious day, but the sun beating down on her and the sticky heat made her feel uncomfortable. Under normal circumstances, she would give up this silly chase and return to the hotel, but she couldn't have Edna gloating later over her inability to keep up. Plus, she felt it was important to contact the unknown woman named Philippa as soon as possible. "Why on earth did he choose to go for a walk down this polluted road when there's a huge air-conditioned shopping centre adjoining the hotel?"

"Perhaps he wanted some air. Even if it's not exactly fresh, it is outdoors. Looks like Horace and Edna have caught up with him. They've got him to stop just ahead." Frederick wasn't a tall man himself, but he had a good eight inches over Marjorie.

"Thank goodness for that," she said.

Moments later, they formed a group of five with the quartet pretending to be intent on getting some fresh air, despite what Marjorie had just said about the pollution.

“Oh look, there’s a café over there. Why don’t we stop for a drink?” She had noticed a square fifty yards ahead with outside tables and some greenery.

“Good idea. Will you join us, Perse?” said Edna. The irritating woman had somehow managed to alter a name that was already shortened, Marjorie assumed, from Percival. Thankfully, Percy took little notice.

“Don’t mind if I do. Too damned hot out here.”

It would help if you removed the jacket and cravat. Not to mention the hat, thought Marjorie, but kept her opinion to herself.

They made their way towards the busy café and found a table in the shade beneath a large beech tree. Horace took charge and explained what food items were on offer as the menu was in Romanian. He needn’t have bothered because there was an English version on the back, but it kept Percy engaged. Horace was his usual smartly dressed self with moustache trimmed to perfection. It wouldn’t surprise Marjorie if he spent hours in front of the mirror each morning, making sure every hair was in place, and she wondered how often he had to tint the moustache and his eyebrows to get them matching the brown of his hair. He looked the image of an English gentleman abroad with his short-sleeved white cotton shirt unbuttoned at the neck. The only part Marjorie felt he could do without was the toupee.

They chatted amicably while deciding what to order from the menu. Marjorie felt it was a little too early for lunch, but the others seemed intent on ordering food, so she opted for Radauti soup. Horace explained this was a tasty chicken and vegetable dish, hugely popular with Romanians and foreigners alike.

“I’d go easy on the vinegar, though. Gives me acid indigestion.”

“Thanks for the tip,” she said.

Horace also ordered the soup for himself. The others chose Romanian meat patties. Marjorie, Edna, and Frederick requested coffee while Horace and Percy had beer.

Once the food and drink were on the table, Edna nudged Marjorie impatiently. Fearing if she didn't broach the subject, Edna might, she obliged.

"Dreadful business about your sister-in-law," Marjorie began cautiously while Percy was chewing on a mouthful of meat. "It must have been an awful shock for your wife and niece."

Wiping his mouth with a napkin, Percy squinted under the dappled sunlight hitting his face. "You're right there. Trust Dolores to make a theatrical exit and God knows what she told that miserable friend of hers – if anything. We can all be grateful to the despicable woman for us being in this predicament. The police won't find anything unusual, you know. Dolores has been abusing cigarettes, booze and medication for years. It was just a matter of time. Sorry, old pal," he looked at Frederick. "Martha said you and Dolores were close once."

"Why would her friend... what was her name again?" Marjorie wanted to keep the conversation on track.

"Philippa, Philippa Trombone. Mouth like a trombone, too. She's the troublemaking best friend. Always stirring."

Marjorie couldn't always remember things straight away, but she knew she would recall that surname.

"Why do you call her a troublemaker?" asked Horace, pushing his empty plate away as the waiter began clearing the table.

"Because she's always causing friction. She didn't want Dolores to come away in the first place, probably because we didn't invite her. This holiday is a treat for my wife. She and Simon share the same birthday, so we thought it would be good to get the gang away together without that interfering busybody. Philippa and Dolores have become closer since Robbie, erm... moved on."

"Do they live near to each other?" Marjorie asked.

"They do now. Or should I say, did? Philippa lives in a village called Wallingford in Oxfordshire. Dolores had a place built just outside the centre when some land came up for sale."

"Can't you call this Mrs Trombone and ask her to retract whatever it was she said to the police?" Frederick suggested.

"Miss, not Mrs. No-one in their right mind would marry Philippa... and as for calling her, there's no point. She wouldn't listen to me, or any of us for that matter. She hates us all. I don't know what got into Martha, ringing her in the first place." Having finished his food, Percy folded his arms, resting them on his belly.

"I expect she felt sorry for her if she and Dolores were close. Do you think this Miss Trombone would listen to a stranger? Would you like me to try? Or Faith perhaps?" Marjorie asked.

Percy released an arm to drain his beer glass before leaning back in his chair. He eyed Marjorie.

"Why would you want to do that?"

"I would have thought it was obvious," chimed in Edna. "So we can all get on with our bloomin' holiday."

"Mm, I wonder? I suppose it wouldn't do any harm trying, and it would save Chloe and Martha the distress of Dolores going through the post-mortem. Philippa might come to her senses if she realises it's not just us she's inconveniencing. Write your number down and I'll text hers to you."

Marjorie almost burst out laughing, but contained herself.

"I, erm..."

"She never carries her mobile and wouldn't know the number if her life depended on it. Hang on a minute," Edna reached into her handbag, withdrawing a business card. "It's old, but the number's still the same. Text it to me."

Percy looked down his nose at the card before grinning.

"I thought your name was Edna?"

"It is. That was my stage name."

Marjorie tried to see the name on the card, but it was impossible as Percy was sitting on the opposite side of the table.

"You can see why I prefer Shakespeare." Percy showed the card to Horace.

"Innocencia Van Gordon?" Horace raised an eyebrow.

Edna snatched the card back. "That name got me many a booking, don't knock it." She stuffed it back in her handbag.

"Edna," Marjorie kicked her under the table. "The number?"

"Oh. All right, but no more comments about the name." She reluctantly passed the card back to Percy.

"I'm getting rather tired," said Marjorie, noticing Percy was about to place the card in his inside jacket pocket, obviously forgetting that moments ago he had offered to text the number immediately. "If you send Miss Trombone's telephone number now, I can make the call as soon as I get back to the hotel."

"Oh, right. Okay, just a minute." Percy donned a pair of reading glasses that appeared from nowhere and examined his phone. After what seemed like an epoch, Edna's phone pinged to the tune of Shirley Bassey's *Big Spender*.

Horace smirked, taking Edna's hand. "I'd like to hear your rendition of that one day."

"Let that be a private performance please," said Marjorie.

"Good luck to you," Percy said, "although the more I think of it, the more I believe you'll be wasting your time. That woman detests us. She won't want to help. I suspect the post-mortem will go ahead, and later on, we'll all be told it was a complete waste of time. Shame Philippa's not here, I don't know whether they have charges over here for wasting police time but I'd have loved to see her charged. Are any of you interested in coming into town?"

"I thought you said you didn't want to go into town earlier?" Frederick almost snapped, but caught himself just in time. Only Marjorie noticed.

“Like Simon, I didn’t want to be dragged around art museums, which would turn into a big shopping trip.”

“I would have thought with your love for Shakespeare, you would like art museums.” Edna’s scorn was unmistakeable.

“The two are mutually exclusive, in my opinion. Art on the stage is what I’m fascinated by. You can keep your Monets and Manets. I’m not interested.”

“You won’t find works by either of those in the art museum here. The paintings are by Romanian and Hungarian artists,” Horace said. “I’ve been a couple of times in the past; bored the socks off me, if I’m honest. The things you have to do in business. Give me avionics and technology any day.”

Marjorie sighed. She herself loved art and would have relished wiling away the afternoon, admiring paintings by artists she no doubt wouldn’t have heard of whose masterpieces she might never have an opportunity to see again, but there was work to be done.

"I'm going to settle my bill and head back to the hotel," she said.

"No, you don't. This one's on me," said Horace. "You go and make your phone call." He winked. "I'll catch up with you shortly."

Under normal circumstances, Marjorie would have protested, but she was in a hurry to find out what Philippa Trombone - what an odd surname - had to say.

"Well done, Marge," Edna sounded breathless with excitement as they walked back to the hotel. Marjorie worried about her sometimes. She had recovered from cancer, but seemed determined to eat herself to death. Still, there were worse ways to die, Marjorie mused.

"What happened to Frederick?" she asked.

"I left him arguing with Horace about who should settle the bill. I do like men who pay, don't you?"

Marjorie exhaled an exasperated breath. She had momentarily sympathised with Edna about the stage name teasing, but one couldn't feel sympathy for the woman for long. There wasn't time to dwell on the dilemma that was Edna, though, as Marjorie was now feeling anxious about calling a total stranger to ask what she had said to the police, and why.

"What are you going to say?" Edna asked.

"I really don't know." Marjorie chuckled. "I expect, being British, I'll start with the weather."

Edna chortled and snorted loudly. "You can be really dry sometimes, you know that, Marge? That's what I like about you. I never know whether you're going to be a snob..."

"Or a yob," finished Marjorie. "And do stop calling me Marge. It's wearing thin."

"I can't help it, it's become a habit, but if it really bothers you, I'll try."

"It does bother me, but I know you won't try, so I suppose I have to live with it."

Edna took Marjorie's arm in a gesture of friendship as they entered the hotel lobby.

Chapter 9

Each time Marjorie picked up the telephone to dial, she put it down again. "I can't concentrate with you hovering so close."

Edna's head appeared next to the handset. "I don't want to miss anything. You might forget something important."

"There's nothing wrong with my memory, but I assure you, if you don't remove that wig from my face, I won't be able to focus at all. It's hard enough having to call somebody I've never met and broach the subject of her conversation with the police without you breathing, quite literally, down my neck!"

Edna stomped to the other side of the room, where she flopped into a comfy chair. “There. Satisfied?”

“As long as you remain there while I make the call. I’ll try to repeat as much of what I can glean without sounding like a parrot. It would be most helpful if you could use the hotel writing paper to take notes.”

Edna’s eyes brightened. “Good thinking. I can do that.”

Once Marjorie was satisfied Edna would give her the space to make the call without interference, she picked up the receiver again. A helpful receptionist who spoke English put the call through. Marjorie’s heart beat a little faster with each ring; she wondered how she was going to handle the situation. Finally, someone picked up.

“Good afternoon, Philippa speaking.” The voice sounded younger than Marjorie had been expecting, but telephone voices could be deceptive. Marjorie hesitated, taking a deep inward breath.

"Hello. Is anyone there?" Philippa Trombone sounded irritated. "Is that you, Martha?" Clearly, she knew the call was coming in from Romania. Edna thrust her head forward with a 'get on with it' nod.

"Good day to you. No, this isn't Martha," Marjorie began. Opting not to mention the weather, she launched straight in. "My name is Lady Marjorie Snellthorpe." She occasionally found the use of her title helpful and hoped this would be one such occasion. "We haven't met before and I am sorry to bother you. I'm calling from Romania."

"I can see that. Are you calling about Dolores?"

"Yes, I am. I'm concerned something odd might be going on here. When I met with Dolores yesterday, before her unfortunate death, she seemed troubled about something." A little white lie couldn't hurt, and 'troubled' could describe the woman storming out of the conference room and humming loudly through the operatic performance. "I overheard Martha Gainsborough's husband mention you this morning and Martha said you were a good friend of the poor woman. When our tour guide mentioned a call from the UK alerting the police with concerns about how Dolores Hagman might have died, I put two and two together."

"I see," Philippa was now the one sounding hesitant. "What's happening over there? I wasn't sure the police were taking me seriously. The officer I spoke with had little grasp of the language."

Marjorie sighed inwardly. Why was it the British expected everyone in the world to speak fluent English while hardly bothering to learn a word of other languages? *Myself included*, she chided herself. *I must make more of an effort, although it's perhaps a little late now.*

"Are you still there?" The impatient voice at the other end of the phone, along with a glare from Edna, prompted Marjorie back to the present.

"Yes, I'm sorry. There's a slight delay on the line. I can assure you, the police are taking you very seriously. The coroner is carrying out a post-mortem on Dolores today, and the police have detained our entire party in Cluj-Napoca until they know the results."

"Brilliant. That's such a relief. But why are they keeping you there? I told them it was her so-called friends and family they needed to watch."

"I couldn't say. I expect it's because we were all present at the opera last evening when your friend's body was discovered. She seemed such a charming person," Marjorie shuddered at the lie and had to look away from Edna, who was pulling faces. "I'm so sorry for your loss."

"Thank you. Dolores and I have been best friends for years. Recently, though, her family and other so-called friends have become more poisonous than usual. They've been trying to split us up. I suppose with that pathetic ex of hers out of the way, they're hoping to get some money from her. Now it appears they might have got their wish, but I won't go down without a fight."

"It's good to know she had such a close friend. I noticed there appeared to be a lot of friction among her party."

"Understatement of the year," muttered Edna.

Marjorie ignored her, continuing, "Are you suggesting someone might have deliberately caused your friend harm? After the paramedics examined her last night, we were told she had suffered a heart attack."

"I'm sure one of them has killed her. They're a bunch of vipers, the lot of them. Don't believe a word any of them tells you, Lady Snellthorpe. Dolores called me last night, telling me she regretted taking the holiday, that she was in fear of her life."

"My goodness. No wonder you called the police."

"What?" Edna hissed from across the room. Marjorie waved a hand for her to be quiet.

"You say Dolores called you and told you she feared for her life? Did she happen to say what or whom she was afraid of?"

"She was scared of all of them. She'd recently come into money, you see. I told her to keep it quiet, but she's always been extravagant, both in spending and in temperament. It didn't take them long to catch on."

"And you believe her coming into money caused tensions within the family and among her friends?"

"No. The tension, as you put it, or rather malice, has always been there. A more unpleasant bunch of people you could never wish to meet. If it turns out to be murder, which I'm sure it will if the police do their job properly..." Philippa's voice cracked and she paused to blow her nose, "...then one of them will have got their way. Don't trust them, especially not the Gainsboroughs."

"But isn't Martha Dolores's sister? Surely you can't be suggesting she would do her any harm? She appeared devastated once she realised Dolores had died, as did her daughter." *And, Martha was also thoughtful enough to telephone to inform you.* Marjorie made sure she didn't speak that thought out loud.

"I'm sure she did. You know they're all would-be thespians. They're great at putting on a show, but that's all it is. A show. That woman had the nerve to call me and tell me the news last night, feigning sympathy. Martha Gainsborough is colder than a freezer in winter. She was positively gloating when she said it was such a pity I hadn't seen Dolores in her last hours." Philippa stopped again, this time letting out a small sob.

"Once again, I'm so sorry for your loss. Thank you for filling me in on the background."

"Why did you call, anyway?" Philippa's tone changed to one of suspicion.

"I wanted to express my condolences. And, as I said earlier, Dolores seemed agitated yesterday. I was concerned."

"She and Martha had a row. Didn't she tell you that?"

"No, she didn't, although I witnessed her leaving after someone at lunch appeared to have said something to upset her."

"That would have been Martha. She was always looking for the opportunity to stick the insults in where they hurt. Typical plain younger sister with no talent. She's insecure. Hasn't got any children, you know; couldn't have them. That was another thing that galled her, so she pawed all over Chloe, vying for her love."

Marjorie was beginning to dislike the woman on the other end of the phone as much as she had disliked Dolores the diva. Perhaps Percy was right and Philippa Trombone was just mischief making.

"I'm sorry. I have to go. My friends are knocking at the door. Do take care, and again, I'm sorry—" Marjorie didn't get to finish the last sentence as she was cut off. Whether by accident or by design, she was uncertain.

"I take it you'd had enough of the conversation," said Edna, "seeing as no-one's knocking at the door."

"Really? I could have sworn I heard a knock," chuckled Marjorie.

"Come on then, Marge. Out with it. I got snippets, but didn't get the complete story. She thinks the sister did it, does she?"

"Why don't we meet with Horace and Frederick and I'll reveal all? It will be better if I don't have to repeat the story multiple times. Philippa Trombone is as nasty as the rest of them, though. I didn't warm to her at all. I hate to admit it, but Percy may have a point."

Marjorie was pleased when Edna went to her room to change into cooler clothes and find a lighter wig – Marjorie assumed she had meant lighter in weight rather than lighter in colour, but one never knew with Edna. The brief respite gave her the opportunity to reflect on the events of the previous day and the words of Philippa Trombone.

She tried to recall the first encounter with Dolores Hagman as the diva had made her dramatic exit from the Picasso room. She remembered Chloe running after her mother, saying, "She didn't mean anything." The 'she', from what Philippa had just said, must have been Martha. Chloe, the downtrodden daughter, appeared closer to her aunt than her mother, but Marjorie could hardly blame her. From what she herself had witnessed, Dolores had treated the poor woman like a skivvy rather than a daughter. Martha, on the other hand, treated her like a friend, and despite what Philippa had said just minutes ago, she had also spoken up for Miss Trombone when Percy had suggested she was stirring. Perhaps Martha was one of those kind people who genuinely tried to see the good in everyone. Admittedly, she was plain to look at, but she and Percy seemed well suited. He listened to her and she was the only one who could counter his behaviour.

What Marjorie couldn't work out was whether Philippa's verbal attack on the party was out of spite, or genuine concern for her friend. Perhaps it was grief. The bit she didn't quite understand was why Dolores, who appeared very much the confident, albeit melodramatic, woman in charge, would be in fear of her life. She had been happily annoying everyone with her loud-cum-louder humming during the first half of the operatic performance, so whatever changed must have happened during the break.

Drat! I should have asked Philippa what time she got the telephone call from Dolores.

An uncomfortable feeling settled on Marjorie's stomach. The only change she could imagine having an effect on the dead woman was the presence of her own newfound friend, whom Dolores had abandoned at the altar. But Dolores had been relaxed – almost high – during the first act of the opera so that couldn't be the reason. Neither could Marjorie imagine Frederick Mackworth deciding to take vengeance on a former fiancée after so many years. It made no sense.

Marjorie stepped onto the balcony overlooking an outdoor area of the hotel for a breath of fresh air. The air was more smoke filled than she would have liked, but air conditioning always made her feel dry. She heard loud shouts coming from a group of youths who were kicking a ball back and forth, then she noticed Denise and Chloe lounging with cocktails in their hands, laughing and joking as if nothing were amiss.

I wonder if Chloe is feeling relief at the loss of her mother more than she feels grief, thought Marjorie.

Moments later, the major appeared in a pair of khaki shorts. The sight of his grey hairs, varicosed legs and knobbly knees would take a little while to shake off. Marjorie laughed, deciding it was time to go in search of Horace, Edna, and Frederick. She almost regretted including Frederick in their investigations until they were certain he had nothing to do with Dolores Hagman's death. After all, his absence during the break and late return for act two were hardly normal behaviour.

The phone in her room shrilled just as she was about to leave. Believing it would be Edna, she returned to answer it.

"Hello."

"I just wanted to say I'd appreciate it if you would keep me informed of any developments. I've just called the police again and they won't tell me anything."

Taken aback for a moment, Marjorie replied, “Is that Philippa?”

“Yes. The receptionist gave me your room number. I realise I’ve probably spoiled your holiday and have no right to ask, but I don’t know what to do with myself. I’ve thought about flying over, but what good would that do? Besides, I hate travelling. Heat doesn’t suit me. I wish I’d joined Dolores now.”

“Were you invited?”

“Not by them, but Dolores asked me to come. She thought it would do me good. I’m almost agoraphobic. She understood. It’s not that easy to flick a switch and leave for a foreign country. I have enough trouble getting out to do my shopping. I try not to let the condition defeat me, but now, without Dolores chivvying me along, I don’t know how I’ll ever cope.”

“I’m not sure how much information we will receive from the police, but I’ll certainly let you know what I can.”

“Thank you. That’s all I ask.”

Just when Marjorie was feeling sorry for the woman, Philippa ruined it by putting the phone down on her again.

It takes little courtesy to say goodbye before ending a call, doesn't it?

Chapter 10

Spending time with Marge Snellthorpe is never boring, Edna thought while changing into lighter clothing and pulling out the only lightweight wig she possessed, which had a purple rinse. She looked at her reflection in the mirror and laughed out loud.

"Marge is going to hate you," she said to the wig as if it were a living entity rather than an inanimate object. She liked to think of all her wigs as living beings, each breathing a special wave of new life into her. It was something she had devised to help her cope with the chemotherapy's destruction of her once-beautiful hair. In her mind, each wig gave her a superpower which prevented her mourning her loss.

She patted the wig in place. This one gave her back her youth. It was like taking an elixir that transported her to the days when she rebelled against her mother's wishes and became a singer. Her mother had been singer herself, but told Edna she didn't wanted her to go through the same hardships she herself had suffered. But to Edna's teenage mind, her mother just wanted to spoil her fun or might have been worried she would be more successful. Edna smiled wistfully into the mirror, remembering the teenage tantrums and arguments. Her mother had worked hard every day of her life to keep Edna and her brother out of poverty, despite her father doing nothing to support the family. When he, a gambler and a womaniser, had been written out of her grandfather's will, it had meant Marge's late husband, Ralph had inherited everything from his father, her uncle. It rarely bothered her these days, particularly when she was rational, but every so often, when she saw how Marge lived, she couldn't help feeling a mild resentment.

And now, she had a lifelong battle against cancer to face. The doctors had told her she was in remission, but these were the same doctors who'd told her that her hair would grow back, and look at how that had gone.

Edna repositioned her wig, patting it again. Both actions helped dispel the morose thoughts. Her mother had been proud of her in the end, and pleased when she married Dennis. Dennis was a good, hardworking man who had put enough by to take her around the world once her cancer treatment ended. But then he'd died.

Edna wiped a tear from her eye. "Stop it, Parkinton. You're stronger than this."

Touching the wig once more, she inhaled the elixir of youth and marched assuredly from her room. The one good thing that had come out of all of her hardships was that she and Marge had rekindled a friendship. They weren't as close as Edna would have liked, but at least they were friends.

Horace and Fred were sitting just inside the coffee bar off the main lobby when Edna arrived downstairs. Horace rose to greet her. Yes, he was a dinosaur, but a nice one. What's more, he appreciated her sense of humour.

He tapped his nose. "Did you find out what the dreaded Philippa Trombone had to say?"

"I overheard snippets, but Marge had a long conversation with her. She'll be down any minute now. I can confirm it was Philippa who called the police and I'm not sure why, but she seems to think Martha had something to do with the diva's death."

"I wish you wouldn't call her that," said Fred.

"And I wish you weren't so soft, but hey, none of us get what we want, do we?"

Fred returned to his sulking.

"Let me get you some coffee," said Horace. "Or would you prefer something stronger?"

"Coffee will do for now, thanks. Watch out, Puffing Percy and Mild Martha are on their way over."

Fred shot her another disapproving look, but the purple wig would not quieten the teenage rebel for him or anyone else.

“Nice hair, by the way,” said Horace.

She gave him a wide grin.

“What have you got, then?” Percy’s manners hadn’t improved any, despite their brunch truce.

“Percy,” Martha gave him a dig in the ribs. “Would you mind us joining you? The girls have gone off somewhere and I think Simon’s resting up in his room.”

“The girls? Oh, you mean Denise and Chloe. I’d hardly call them girls, but whatever you say. We’re just about to order hot drinks.”

“In that case, we could have some tea,” said Martha, flashing her husband a warning look which told him – and Edna – he wasn’t to say anything else without permission.

Odd relationship between those two, thought Edna. He was a bad-tempered man with an apparently meek and mild wife who definitely wore the trousers.

"Suit yourself." Edna wasn't keen on the couple staying while she still hadn't heard what her cousin had to say. At this rate, Marge would forget everything the Trombone woman had told her.

Ignoring the lack of welcome, Martha ordered tea and she and Percy took seats opposite Fred. Horace and Edna shared an ample sofa. Martha sipped her tea with decorum, while Percy screwed his nose up.

"Can't stand this weak dishwater. I don't know what they put in it, but it's not tea."

"The coffee's marvellous, though," said Horace, pouring himself and Edna drinks from a large pot. Frederick said nothing.

"I'll take your word for it. I never touch the stuff. Doctor's orders; he told me it's bad for my blood pressure."

Fred half-grinned, shooting Edna a 'told you so' look.

“Percy said you were going to phone Philippa.” Martha was attempting to sound casual, but Percy’s beetroot face said otherwise.

“Marge was.”

Percy could obviously hold himself back no longer. “So what did the old boot have to say?”

“Percy! Behave.”

“Sorry. It’s this blasted heat… and this… excuse they call tea.”

“Forgive my husband. He hates flying, doesn’t like hot weather and detests anything unusual.”

“And yet he’s flown all over Europe acting in Shakespearian plays,” said Edna, rolling her eyes.

“Hardly. He’s done a few, but not for many years. He’s put on a bit of weight in recent times, which makes getting enough seat and legroom difficult when we travel.”

Edna looked at Percy and felt a little sympathy for the first time. She had also packed on the weight over the past few decades, and once it was on, there was no taking it off.

“Marge doesn’t like the tea here either,” she said.

“Talking of whom, here’s your cousin now,” said Horace.

Chapter 11

By the time Marjorie found the trio in the coffee bar, she discovered they already had company. Percy and Martha Gainsborough had also made themselves comfortable around a large table.

“There you are, Marge.” Edna spoke as if they had been waiting for hours when, judging by the fresh tea and coffee pots with almost full cups, they couldn’t have been there for more than fifteen minutes.

“As you can see,” she replied, trying not to stare at the purple hair. *Where does she find these wigs?* “Good afternoon,” Marjorie addressed Percy and Martha.

"Did you get anywhere with your phone call?" asked Percy. His round face appeared flushed, possibly from his recent exertion. Perhaps he had only just got back to the hotel after his trip into the city centre. Marjorie felt momentarily confused, but then remembered it was he who had given them Philippa's telephone number in the first place. That explained why he had sat with the others.

"I can't say I did, unfortunately."

"What did the old bat have to say? I told the wife you wouldn't get very far with her."

"Just what you already suspected. She told me it was she who called the police last night, although she was surprised we had all been detained. I think she assumed it would just be your party, but why she imagined that would be the case, I don't know."

"I expect she was hoping we'd be the ones because we knew Dolores best. Having said that, Frederick here also knew her," said Martha pointedly.

"She's still convinced someone did Dolores in, is she?" Percy asked before snorting.

"To be honest, I'm uncertain what Philippa Trombone thinks. I believe she was very fond of your wife's sister, however." Marjorie fixed her eyes on Martha, who appeared uncomfortable under her gaze, dropping her own eyes.

"They were good friends, but I can't understand why she's cast this shadow over our holiday."

"Surely it's the death of your sister that's cast a shadow?" said Edna. "I don't have a sister, but I've got a brother and I'd be devastated if something happened to him. I don't think I could go on as if nothing had happened." Edna's tone was accusatory.

"You know nothing about it," snapped Percy. "Dolores Hagman was unbearable in life and now she's become insufferable in death. If it weren't for my wife's loyalty to her niece, we wouldn't have had anything to do with the woman."

So Martha is the doting aunt. At least that part of Philippa's story was true, thought Marjorie.

"Now, now, old fellow," said Horace. "Let's try not to speak ill of the dead before they're cold in the grave, eh? I'm superstitious about these things."

Percy mopped his beady brow and picked up a mug of tea. "Fair enough, but it's hard to find anything good to say about that woman."

"Percy and Dolores never got on," explained Martha. "My sister could be difficult, but she wasn't all bad. Dolores had a lot to deal with over the past few years when her career dried up along with her marriage… you know… breaking up. She'd always drunk heavily, but it's been a lot worse over recent months. Then she took up smoking again; my sister hadn't smoked for ten years. Although recently I thought things were looking up. We all felt she'd turned a corner."

"Really? In what way?" asked Horace.

"She came into money, then started lording it over everyone. No longer the pathetic ex opera singer, she became lady of the manor." Percy couldn't resist another dig.

"Was it an inheritance?" Marjorie had forgotten to ask Philippa where the money had come from.

"I don't think so," said Martha. "It was all a bit odd, actually. She wouldn't admit to anything, but it was clear from her spending and the change in her circumstances that money was involved. No-one in the family has died recently and I can't think of anyone else who would have left my sister money."

"Doesn't her daughter know where it came from?" Edna pressed, eyes squinting.

"I didn't feel I could ask and she didn't say," Martha replied.

More like you did ask and she wouldn't say, thought Marjorie.

"But none of this has anything to do with her death," snapped Percy. "The woman was a heart attack waiting to happen."

Not too unlike you, thought Marjorie, noting again how red his face was and more sweat having to be wiped from his forehead. She didn't mention her thoughts, but said instead, "I expect we'll find out soon enough. It's getting late."

Percy checked his watch. "You're right. Come on, Martha, let's change for dinner. Whatever the outcome, we're stuck here for another night. We might as well enjoy the food."

Marjorie waited until they were out of earshot. "Did they say anything else that might help us?"

"Nothing much," said Horace. "They were fishing for whatever Philippa Trombone had told you. Why does that pleasant woman put up with a man like that?"

"Some people love their husbands." Frederick spoke for the first time since Marjorie had joined them. He had the faraway look in his eyes again. What was it that made her want to put everything right for him?

"And some husbands don't deserve it," said Horace.

Marjorie remembered something about Horace's background. He'd had an affair while his wife was pregnant and his sons never forgave him – something like that, but she might be mixing him up with someone else.

"Come on then, Marge. What did *Miss* Trombone really say?" Edna brought her mind back to the present.

"She said that Dolores had called her last evening and told her she regretted coming on holiday and that she was fearful. 'In fear for her life', was how Philippa put it. So when she got the news of Dolores's death, she called the police and passed on what her friend had told her."

"And do you believe she was telling the truth?" asked Horace.

"It's hard to say. She's rather embittered herself, and had nothing good to say about any of the family or friends. She even said Martha called her to gloat.

"I think we can assume Dolores called Philippa – the police would have checked the dead woman's mobile phone records at the very least, though whatever was actually said, we won't know what happened until we get the results of the post-mortem. Philippa also said what Martha – or was it Percy? – just confirmed: that Dolores had come into money recently."

"Did she tell you where the money came from?" Edna quizzed.

"You were there listening to the conversation. I didn't ask."

"Oh, Marge, I knew I should have made the call."

Marjorie doubted Edna's roughshod way of questioning would have got her very far with Philippa Trombone, but she held her peace.

"It's not the sort of thing one asks a new acquaintance, and I didn't want her to get suspicious. It must have seemed odd as it was, a stranger calling her from Romania."

"Quite right," said Horace. "Keep your hair on, Edna."

Edna chortled, straightening her permed purple wig. "You'd better do the same," she replied. Horace's hand went to his toupee, which was still where it should be. He laughed loudly.

"Touché."

"The only other thing I gleaned from Philippa Trombone was that Martha is close to Chloe, but I think we could see that already, and Percy just confirmed that was the reason for their staying in touch with Dolores. The call was almost a waste of time, except, if Philippa is telling the truth, Dolores Hagman may well have been murdered."

"A sombre thought," said Horace.

Frederick put his head in his hands. "And I'm going to be prime suspect."

"Why?" asked Marjorie.

"Because, as your cousin-in-law reminded me just this morning, I was the jilted bridegroom."

Frederick jumped up from his seat, turned away and marched towards the lifts as if he wanted to run away. They all gawped after him.

"Poor chap. Not much of a holiday for him, is it? First, he bumps into his runaway bride. Next, he's likely to go to the top of the Romanian coppers' must-have-dunnit list." Horace drained his coffee cup.

"Then it's up to us to prove he didn't," said Marjorie.

"But what if he did, Marge? Fred was the last one in after the performance break. He says he was in the foyer, but we didn't see him. He might have been harbouring vengeful feelings for years, and then, what do you know? There she is, the cause of all his heartache, behaving as if they'd never met."

Marjorie sipped her tea. "And how do you suppose he killed her and made it look like a heart attack?"

"Didn't someone say he married a doctor? He could have picked up all sorts of tips," said Edna.

"On how to heal people rather than how to kill them, I would have thought. I don't believe

Frederick capable of killing anyone. You've seen him. He's harmless; lost, almost."

"Marjorie," Edna's use of her full name grabbed her attention, "we only met him yesterday. We don't know what he's capable of." Edna's sympathy was worse than her teasing. Marjorie found herself blinking away a tear as she answered.

"May I point out that we've only known that motley crew for twenty-four hours too, but I have no trouble believing any one of them capable of murder. Plus, their history with Dolores goes back decades. They have shown how openly hostile and dysfunctional they are."

Horace nodded. "Marjorie's right, you know, but we need to keep an open mind regarding Fred. I suggest we give him as little information as possible."

Marjorie placed her cup on the table. "I can go along with that."

"What I don't understand is why any of her mob would do her in now. Surely they could have done it at any time?" Edna argued. "And why in Romania?"

"It makes sense to me. They chose a foreign country in which they believed the police would be too lax to investigate. Poison would be the most likely weapon, and whoever killed her knew she would go outside for a cigarette. I suspect they bided their time planning the murder, choosing something that would make her death look like a heart attack.

"As for the now, don't you see? It must be to do with this extra money. I expect Chloe stands to inherit, so she must be top of the list. She's shown little in the way of grief and wasn't at all concerned when her mother didn't come back to her seat after the halftime break. I saw her and Denise Jeffries drinking cocktails and laughing outside before I came down here. And Chloe's mother treated her like a skivvy."

"I can't argue with that, we all witnessed it for ourselves," said Edna. "But being relieved someone has died, especially if she thinks it was natural causes, is different to killing them. That poor woman hasn't got it in her."

Marjorie was about to say that neither had Frederick, but they would be back to the argument that they hadn't known either of these people for long enough to make an objective judgement. She was pleased to see Faith Weathers heading in their direction.

"Any news?" asked Horace as Faith sat down.

"The post-mortem is almost done and they're saying nothing so far. They're doing some more tests. Fingers crossed we'll be off in the morning. I was told we'll get a telephone call if there's nothing suspicious, but I wouldn't be surprised if the inspector I spoke to this morning comes in person as he needs an interpreter."

"The uniformed officer I saw leave with him this morning?" Marjorie surmised.

"Precisely. So don't assume anything's amiss if they turn up later."

"Couldn't he just let the officer who speaks English telephone?" Horace asked.

"He might well do that. It was hard to understand what the man I spoke to was saying. We just need to be patient for a while longer. But they can't have found anything so far, otherwise they would have said so. At least, I hope they would have."

Edna sighed. "Not very reassuring, I must say."

Marjorie shot Edna a warning look before turning to Faith. "Thank you for letting us know. And as you say, we might be able to put all this behind us in the morning and get on with our trip. I'm so looking forward to spending some time in Bucharest. I'm told it's a beautiful city."

"It is," said Horace.

"Don't tell us," teased Edna, "you've been there on business."

"They do have aeroplanes in Romania, you know," he said, teasing back. "Now, I think we deserve a drink. What say we go to the bar and order something a little stronger than coffee?"

"I'm in. Are you coming, Marge?"

"I'll be along shortly. I just want to ask Faith something."

"What shall we get you?" asked Horace.

"A glass of white wine, please."

"We'll see you in a minute," said Edna.

After they had left, Marjorie turned to Faith. "Are you given much information about guests before they travel?"

"What sort of information?"

"I was thinking about health, medication, criminal records, that sort of thing."

"Not the criminal past, but yes, there are health forms to be completed. Not that people are always honest. Why?"

"I'm just wondering if any of our guests take medication that could cause a person to have a heart attack if accidentally ingested."

"I tell you what, I'll look into it, but I won't be able to share anything confidential."

"Unless the post-mortem finds one such medication in the victim's system, of course," said Marjorie, collecting her handbag and leaving Faith to ponder.

Chapter 12

The atmosphere over dinner was tense as the guests still hadn't heard the outcome of the post-mortem. Martha Gainsborough had been doing her best to keep a lid on tempers threatening to erupt. Her husband Percy would be the most likely to explode, from what Marjorie had observed, but she couldn't have been more wrong. She had just laid down her knife and fork and picked up a glass of red wine when the outburst Martha had tried so hard to prevent came from an unexpected source.

Denise Jeffries slammed her cutlery down, flicked her mousy brown hair back aggressively, and yelled, "This is absolutely ridiculous. I'm supposed to be on holiday, so why is it I feel like a prisoner? Surely, the authorities should have sorted the autopsy results by now. They have no right keeping us waiting like this."

On hearing the outburst, guests sitting at surrounding tables gazed at the red-faced woman with the flashing dark blue eyes, some in horror, some in amusement. A couple nearby tutted loudly and people at a crowded table muttered their disapproval.

"I'm sure we'll hear something soon, darling." It was the first time since Marjorie had met him that Major Jeffries appeared embarrassed. "Why don't we go to the bar and get a drink?"

"You think that's a cure for everything, Dad. I don't want to go to the bar and I don't want a drink," Denise yelled. "I want answers."

Marjorie was extremely relieved to see Faith heading in their direction. She gave Denise a glare before saying, "I didn't want to disturb you during dinner, but if you're happy to skip desserts, you can join me in the usual conference room and I'll let you know what's happening."

Not waiting another moment, Denise leapt out of her chair and stomped from the restaurant, heels clacking on the wooden floor.

"I must apologise for my daughter," said the major. "I'm afraid she has a wild temper. Too much like me, I fear. Her mother was the only one who could calm her when she got like this."

Marjorie watched Frederick and the major depart, the latter less self-assured than usual, with Faith. The rest of the Hagman party followed quickly, muttering and murmuring in their disgust.

"Come on, Marge, don't you want to know what's going on?" Edna nudged her.

"I do indeed, but I will not make an undignified departure, nor associate myself with what just happened. I shall finish this rather excellent wine. I'm sure Faith will wait for us."

"Quite right," said Horace. "Appalling behaviour. I'm not eating with that lot again, far too tense for my liking." He drained his brandy glass.

After a suitable pause, during which the other guests had returned their attention to their meals, Marjorie made to rise. A waiter appeared behind her and pulled her chair back. She had feared Edna would be frustrated at being kept waiting for answers, but it seemed even her brusque cousin-in-law could show decorum when necessary.

When they arrived in the Picasso room, the usual loud voices greeted them. Faith wasn't alone. The inspector from the morning and the uniformed officer were being bombarded with questions and insults, but seemingly weren't giving anything away.

"About time too! That's the second time you lot have kept us waiting," Percy snapped. Marjorie ignored the proverbial daggers firing from the still crimson-faced Denise and took a seat. Horace and Edna also sat down.

Faith began, “I’m afraid I have some bad news, but also some that’s slightly more positive. Not that anything is great under these circumstances.” She hesitated, clearly not sure how to make her announcement.

“Get on with it, then,” Percy barked. The inspector, who Marjorie noticed had been studying the audience, scowled at Percy.

“His card is marked,” she whispered to Edna.

“So it should be. Nasty bloke. Who does he think he is?”

“It now appears that Mrs Dolores Hagman died from cyanide poisoning,” Faith declared, offering a look of sympathy to Chloe. Mumbling and muttering spread around the table while the news sank in. Marjorie saw the inspector was still watching them all closely.

“It could be all those cigarettes she’s been smoking. I warned her chain smoking would kill her in the end,” said Percy. “I read you can get cyanide poisoning from too much smoking.”

"The cyanide was ingested," the uniformed police officer announced.

More murmuring.

"Are you suggesting the lady was murdered, or was it some kind of accident?" Horace cut to the chase. "Did anyone else take ill on the night of the opera?"

The officer spoke in Romanian to the inspector, who shook his head.

"So, you're implying someone around this table is a killer?" The major had found his authoritative voice.

"The police are keeping an open mind and will conduct further enquiries," said Faith. "In the meantime, we've been given permission to leave for Bucharest tomorrow once we've all given statements." She was clearly trying to sound positive.

"That's something at least," said Chloe. "Can we go now, please?"

"Yes. Inspector Radu would like you all to meet in the lobby after breakfast in the morning. He has commandeered this room for interviews and to take statements."

The Hagman party couldn't leave fast enough, bustling towards the door, probably for fear of being arrested at any moment. Frederick appeared stunned; a pallor settled on his face, and with no hair, he looked as close to a ghost as Marjorie was ever likely to see. Marjorie patted him on the forearm.

"You may leave, Mr Mackworth," instructed the young police officer. "The inspector would like to speak to the rest of you before you go."

If Frederick was shocked at his companions being kept behind, he didn't show it. He got up, wringing his shaking hands, and headed for the door.

Faith turned to the inspector. "I'll leave you to it."

After everyone had left, the uniformed officer closed the door before she and the inspector sat down. "I'm Danielle Hatmanu. This is Inspector de Politie Radu. He's the same rank as detective inspector in your language. I expect you're wondering what you're doing here?"

Danielle had twinkly brown eyes and wore her uniform with pride, Marjorie noticed. The inspector's eyes were much more serious.

"Indeed, we are," said Marjorie. "Perhaps you would be so kind as to enlighten us."

"From our conversations with Mrs Weathers..." *Ms*, thought Marjorie, but didn't correct her, "... and through our own background checks, we are certain that you three had no contact with the dead woman or her party prior to meeting yesterday?"

"That's right," Horace confirmed.

"Inspector Radu would like you to know that none of you are under suspicion."

"I should think not," said Edna, adjusting the blonde wig she had donned for the evening. It had relieved Marjorie not to see the purple number make a second appearance when they had met for pre-dinner drinks.

"However..."

"Oh dear. There's always a however," said Marjorie, to which Danielle smiled warmly.

"...I'm the only one on our team who speaks English, and it's not perfect. We understand from your history, Mr Tyler, that you speak fluent Romanian."

"I'm a bit rusty, but yes, I do," Horace answered.

Edna's eyes were on stalks and Marjorie felt her own eyebrows almost reaching her hairline. Horace had been coy about his command of the language, leaving her wondering at his being unusually bashful.

"Although we would still like to take statements from you all, Inspector Radu requests that you, Mr Tyler, sit in on the interviews and assist if I have difficulty understanding anything," Danielle continued.

Marjorie wondered if the request was negotiable, but doubted it.

"Well, as I said, I'm a little rusty, but should be fluent enough to help out if you get stuck."

"Get stuck?" quizzed Danielle.

"Yes... have difficulty understanding," explained Horace.

Danielle grinned. "There, you see, you're helping already." She spoke to the inspector again in Romanian and he nodded. "There is one other thing," said Danielle.

"Just a minute," interrupted Edna, turning on Horace, "you never said you were fluent in the language."

"Did you not notice how he was able to have a telephone conversation with a Romanian, and then speak to the emergency services last night?" Marjorie wished Edna would pay more attention to others, but she herself wondered what the history the police officer had alluded to was.

"It didn't seem relevant and you never asked," said Horace. "As a matter of fact, my mother was half Romanian."

He looked down at his hands. Something told Marjorie that Horace had a past he'd rather not discuss.

Horace pivoted back to Danielle. "What's the other thing?"

"Mrs Weathers told us that the three of you had solved a murder mystery on a previous outing."

"And you would like us to keep our noses out?"

Horace translated Marjorie's meaning into Romanian.

"In one way, yes, and in another, no. You can get close to our suspects without arousing suspicion, so we would like you to report anything you see or overhear that might help us find the killer. But," she quickly checked with Inspector Radu, "we do not want you taking any undue risks or trying to solve this crime alone."

"Humph. We do the work, you get the glory," said Edna. Danielle appeared confused. Horace showed his fluency by translating the meaning of Edna's complaint.

Danielle grinned once more. She had an open, friendly face, unblemished by the work she undertook, reminding Marjorie of her good friend, Detective Constable Rachel Prince.

"We would appreciate it if you could report anything you discover back to us. Inspector Radu and myself will join you in Bucharest while the team here continues to make enquiries and speaks to people who attended the opera."

"We would be happy to help in any way we can," said Marjorie.

The inspector said something in Romanian and Marjorie recognised Frederick's name being mentioned. This time, Horace translated.

"He doesn't want Frederick Mackworth knowing anything about us assisting. They've been told of his past with the dead woman and don't want to take any chances. Obviously, everyone will know about me sitting in on the interviews, but other than that, we're going to have to exclude him. I'm sorry," he looked at Marjorie.

Frederick is not a murderer, Marjorie wanted to shout. But she said nothing. If the police thought she was fond of him, they might withdraw their request for help, and she didn't want that. The only way to prove Frederick's innocence was by going along with his exclusion for now.

"Of course," she said finally. "We hardly know Mr Mackworth anyway; we only met him at the airport yesterday morning."

Edna threw her a look of disdain before asking, "Who told you about his history with the diva, then?"

Horace interpreted as Danielle appeared tired and unable to get to grips with Edna's northern accent. The inspector replied.

"It seems Denise was having a good go at Fred before we arrived, saying he was a bad omen. Danielle... erm, Officer Hatmanu asked her to explain what she meant by that and she was delighted to oblige, as were the rest of the party." Horace again looked at Marjorie. "The police don't believe he's a strong candidate for the murder, but they have to consider the fact that Dolores threw him over."

"Indeed. I wouldn't expect anything else. Are we free to go now?" Marjorie asked.

"Yes," said Danielle. "We'll interview you three first thing in the morning, then we can start on the rest of the group. I'm afraid it might be a long day for you all."

"How do you think the cyanide was ingested?" Marjorie asked.

"It was most probably via a hot drink. They found a flask close to the body which the pathologist has taken samples from. We believe it belonged to Mrs Hagman. Someone must have tampered with it before she left the hotel."

"Or during the break," said Marjorie. Danielle explained what she had said to the inspector, who replied, eyeing Marjorie closely as he spoke. Horace, it appeared, was getting into his stride with interpreting now.

"He says you are very astute, Lady Marjorie."

Edna harrumphed once more. “I don’t know about you, but I need a drink.”

“Goodnight, Inspector. Goodnight, Danielle,” said Marjorie. Horace said goodnight in Romanian and they followed a disgruntled Edna.

Once at the bar, she complained, “I hope this doesn’t mean we’re going to be held indefinitely in Bucharest when we get there. I’m looking forward to getting on the river again. It’s too hot on land. Even my lightweight wig made my head sweat. It’s all right for you, Marge, you like this sort of thing.”

Marjorie’s momentary sympathy evaporated as quickly as it had arrived.

“Whatever gives you that idea?”

“The sparkle in your eyes when they asked for our help, that’s what. I’m more observant than you give me credit for, even though *you’re very astute, Lady Marjorie*.”

Edna’s sarcasm didn’t go unnoticed by Horace. “Come on, team. We need to work together. Let me buy you both a drink. And remember, Edna, we're not under suspicion, so if they detain anyone, it will be that unpleasant lot, not us."

"Mine's a Scotch," said Edna.

Marjorie welcomed Horace's intervention. He really was growing on her. There was a lot more to him than just a flirty old man.

Chapter 13

Following her own interview the next morning, Marjorie didn't know what to do with herself. She had asked Horace to meet her and Edna as soon as the police were finished with him, but she suspected that would be a long time coming. It was vital for them to share any information while it was still fresh if they were going to find out who had killed Dolores Hagman.

She found a comfortable seat in the small café area just off the lobby which served hot and cold drinks and ordered a pot of coffee. It would be a good place to wait for Edna to emerge from her interview. The inspector was conducting the interviews in the Picasso Conference Room, which by now they had become intimately acquainted with.

Marjorie saw Faith sitting in the lobby speaking on her mobile phone, no doubt giving an update to her fellow guide in Bucharest or to her employers. Faith waved and motioned she would join her in a moment, so Marjorie ordered an extra pot of coffee. Coffee wasn't her usual drink; tea was by far her preference, but somehow the tea in the hotel didn't taste right. At least with coffee, it didn't matter where one was in the world. The beans gave off the same familiar bitter taste. Tea, for her, had to be brewed in a certain way to make it taste just right. The water also played an important role in the eventual result. Something was amiss with both in the Platinia, she felt. Besides, Romania was a coffee-drinking nation, so she understood why the hotel wasn't serving tea in the way she would like.

"All sorted." Faith sat in one of the comfy chairs, knees together with heels tucked in to one side, just as the second pot of coffee arrived "Is that for me?"

"I took the liberty of ordering for you. I don't expect you've had much time for refreshments."

"That's so thoughtful, Marjorie. Thank you." Faith poured herself a mug of black coffee.

"I take it by all sorted, you mean our onward travel arrangements?"

"Yes. All the internal flights were fully booked for the next few days. It appears there's a huge sporting event taking place in Bucharest, but I've booked us on the night train. I'm afraid I could only get one two-bed sleeper, two four-beds and a single. I'm hoping the men will agree to bunk in together. That leaves the three remaining women from the Hagman party taking the other four-bedder. Would you be happy to share with Edna for the one night?"

"Happy's not the word I'd use. But if it helps even things out, I'm sure I'll manage. Perhaps I won't hear the snoring above the sound of the train." Marjorie doubted she would get a wink of sleep, but at least if Horace and Frederick would be in with Percy and the major, they might find out something.

“Thank you, Marjorie. Under the circumstances, it seemed the best of the available options.” Faith drained her coffee cup. Worry lines smothered her forehead.

“Is there something else bothering you, dear?”

“I suppose I’m not relishing the idea of being on the same train as a killer. Especially in a cabin by myself.”

“That’s easily remedied. We can swap places.” Marjorie chuckled. Noting the hesitancy, she continued, “I’m joking, but I don’t believe you have anything to fear. The murder was personal, not random. None of us are targets.”

“But how can you be certain? Oh, I’m sorry, Lady Snellthorpe, I shouldn’t even be sharing these thoughts with you. It’s just, I feel I’ve gotten to know you.”

“Then stick with Marjorie, please, and don’t hesitate to share your worries. It’s a heavy load you've had to carry over the past couple of days. I understand."

"Understand what, Marge?" The booming voice of her cousin-in-law cut through the comfortable moment.

"I was just saying to Faith I understand it can't be helped that I have to share a sleeper cabin with you on an overnight train tonight."

Edna grinned widely. "Wonderful. We can have a girly talk. We've hardly spent any time together since we got here."

Just the way I like it, thought Marjorie. "What on earth is *girly* talk when it's at home? Act your age, Edna."

"You know exactly what it is, and why should I? I refuse to feel old, and so should you."

On this point, Marjorie fully agreed, but pride prevented her from admitting it. "Now Faith has managed to book us on the overnight to Bucharest, at least we'll be on the move again."

"Not a minute too soon, if you ask me. I'll be glad to be rid of that lot." Edna inclined her head towards the sofas in the lobby where the five remaining members of the Hagman party were waiting to be called. "Oh, I almost forgot, I was to ask that horrible major's daughter to go in next. She seemed all right yesterday when she was telling me and Horace jokes about Percy's exploits but talk about split personality. What's her name again?"

"Denise," said Faith. "Don't worry, I'll tell her. I need to let them know about our travel plans for tonight. I can only hope they'll comply." Faith left the two of them and strode across the lobby, a woman on a mission.

"What did she mean by the comply business? Is there any coffee in that pot?"

"She's going to ask the men to share a four berth and the women to share another. And yes, there is coffee in the pot, but you will need a fresh mug or cup and saucer."

"Don't tell me Faith has to share with those women?"

"Not at all. She needs some privacy. She has a single."

"It's as well for some," muttered Edna while waving a hand at a waiter who came to offer assistance.

"What can I get you?" he asked.

"A fresh cup and saucer and one of those delicious cinnamon pastries. Do you want one, Marge?"

"No, thank you."

"Horace is enjoying himself in there. He and the inspector are having a right laugh in between the young 'un asking questions."

"While we're on the subject, I have had little opportunity to ask you before. Did you or Horace notice anything unusual on the night in question?"

Edna paused while the waiter left her crockery and pastry before answering. "Nothing much I can remember. I had a conversation with Martha after the late lunch we had, and she openly admitted she and her sister weren't all that close. I think I told you Dolores was seven years older. The other thing she said was that she'd never met Fred. Dolores met him in Bath or Bristol, somewhere like that."

"I thought I detected a West Country accent from Frederick," said Marjorie.

"Martha said she and her parents lived in Norwich and Dolores didn't go home much. She reacted a bit when I mentioned Fred being melancholic, said she'd suffered from depression around that time. Do you think any of that's relevant?"

"Other than her not getting on with her sister, I don't think so. Odd, she hadn't met Frederick, though. I wonder if that means they didn't invite her to the wedding.

"You're right, Marge. Fancy not inviting your own sister to your wedding. Unless it had something to do with Martha's mental state back then."

"Indeed, that could explain it. Now think back to the night of the opera. You and Horace were among the first to leave and the last to return before Frederick. Did you see anything of the others while you were in the foyer?"

Edna took a large bite from the pastry and sat back, chewing, eyes scrunched. “The first thing we both did was go to the toilets. None of ’em were in there. I passed the major heading for the gents on my way out. I also think I saw that snotty geezer heading outside for a smoke.”

“Percy Gainsborough?”

“Yeah, him.”

“What makes you think he was going for a smoke?”

“The cigar in his hand gave me a clue.”

“So, that’s two people we know went outside as well as Dolores.”

“Who’s the other one?”

“The major. Remember, Frederick mentioned it the night of the opera, after we’d got back. He said he saw the major coming in from outside. Did you see Percy come back inside?”

“No, but he must have, because he was there for the second half.” Edna giggled, clearly enjoying herself.

"Quite. Who else did you see?"

"Horace."

Marjorie sighed. "Don't be facetious. As well as Horace?"

"It's a bit hazy after that. Horace's Scotch had a real kick to it... he probably remembers better than me. He can hold his drink."

"So you don't remember seeing any of the women at all. Typical—"

"What do you mean by that?"

Marjorie didn't answer. There was no point. "I was one of the last to leave the auditorium and I didn't see very much at all. The major and Percy Gainsborough must be our primary focus to begin with. What were they doing outside and why haven't either of them mentioned it?"

"They might well have discussed where they all were with their friends. I think we need to wait and see what Horace has to say later. It's good we've got an inside man, isn't it?"

"It should help as long as he relates facts rather than embellishing their stories."

"He does like to paint a picture, you're right there. I know you don't want to think about it, Marge, but it could still have been Fred."

Marjorie was about to snap, but recognised the concern in Edna's brown eyes. "And if it was Frederick we'll find out. The thing is, if Dolores took her own flask into the auditorium, it was most likely tampered with here at the hotel or during transit. And who saw what and where on the evening of the opera could lead us down a worthless rabbit hole. The police didn't ask me about my movements prior to going to the opera at all."

"Well, they wouldn't, would they? We're not on the suspect list. We didn't know the woman – thank God. I'm sure they'll take when the flask might have been tampered with into account."

"Are we certain it was her flask?" Marjorie checked.

"Her daughter confirmed it was. I asked that nice Danielle. Apparently, Dolores took it everywhere, often full of liquor, but on the night in question it was filled with vanilla hot chocolate."

"Another mystery solved," said Marjorie.

"Why she didn't taste the cyanide, I presume you mean." Edna polished off the rest of her pastry.

"Indeed. I understand cyanide has an almond taste, but I imagine it would be difficult to distinguish in a flavoured hot chocolate. It only takes a small amount of the poison to give a person a heart attack. Hence the initial conclusion that was the way a woman of her age, with her smoking and drinking history, would most likely have died. The important questions have to be who killed her, why kill her and why now?"

"You said before it had to be about this recent influx of money. I suggest we need to find out where that money came from. The best person to ask about that is Chloe, seeing as Martha said she didn't know where it had come from."

"I handed Horace a list of questions to bring up with Inspector Radu. That question was top of the list."

"You never fail to amaze me, Marge," said Edna. "Body's wearing down a bit, but your mind's as sharp as a razor, ain't it?"

"That's a backhanded compliment if ever I heard one. Nevertheless, thank you. Do you think we should join the four remaining suspects while Denise Gainsborough is being interviewed? Faith seems to have left them to it." Marjorie observed Percy and Major Jeffries having a heated discussion while Martha and Chloe sat close together on a sofa. They could almost be mother and daughter.

That idea went through Marjorie's mind, jolting her brain into overdrive. Edna broke through the train of thought.

"Do we have to? I can't think of anything worse. Besides, I was thinking of going to that big shopping complex attached to the hotel. I need a new wig. The brunette's losing its shine... don't look at me like that, Marge. You have no idea how difficult it is to keep me 'air looking glam."

"You could try taking better care of a single one of them. You're exasperating sometimes, Edna. Actually, though, it might be a good idea to give them a wide berth until later. We need to act naturally. I don't want them to suspect we're investigating Dolores Hagman's death. You go shopping. I'll sit here and watch the world go by."

"Are you sure you don't want to come? We could have lunch out."

"Quite sure, thank you. You enjoy yourself. If you're not back for lunch, we can catch up later. Faith seemed to expect the interviews to go on for hours."

"Don't you think you're being a bit obvious, Marge?"

"I don't know what you mean."

"You're waiting for your fancy man, Fred. Admit it, you're soft on him."

"His name is Frederick, and don't be so ridiculous! I like him and I'm intrigued to know more about him, but that's it. Unlike you, I'm not looking for a replacement husband."

Marjorie regretted her outburst as soon as she had said it. Edna recoiled, pain momentarily flashing through her eyes.

"Have it your way. I'll see you later."

Marjorie nodded, not trusting herself to say anything else. As she watched Edna storm off, she knew what she had said had been hurtful and uncalled for. She was well aware how much Edna missed her late husband, just as she still missed Ralph despite the years passing. Why had she reacted so? She could usually control her emotions. Edna would say it was because she'd hit a nerve, and maybe she had, but Marjorie had meant it when she said she wasn't seeking a husband.

Companionship – now that was another matter altogether. She detected a kindred spirit in Frederick, although they had only just met. He brought something out in her she didn't quite understand. Perhaps it was as well the police had suggested they keep their distance – at least in terms of the investigation. Edna had been right about one thing: Marjorie had been half looking out for Frederick all morning after he didn't show up for breakfast. This really wouldn't do at her age.

Chapter 14

Beginning to wish she had gone shopping with Edna, Marjorie felt the hours drag by and she was itching to know what Horace had discovered. As the morning had worn on, the police officers had summoned a few more of the Hagman party for their interviews. Marjorie wondered why she was still sitting in the same place. Frederick hadn't appeared downstairs at all, so she could only assume he was moping in his room.

It's time to take action, she concluded, having observed each person before and after their interview. None of them, from what she could gather, was giving anything away, although it was difficult to determine much from where she was sitting. They were clearly quizzing each other as each returned to their seat, but she couldn't hear anything they were saying.

Just as Marjorie was about to put the book she had been pretending to read away and head over to join the group, Major Jeffries stopped by, having just been interviewed.

"Do you mind if I join you? I'm a bit sick of my lot."

"Please do," said Marjorie, putting the book down on the table.

"It's a complete waste of time, all of this. I can't see why they don't just leave us alone."

"They can't really, can they? They have to investigate when a woman has been poisoned."

"So they say, but it wouldn't surprise me if Dolores did herself in. Has anyone thought of that, eh? Well, they have now, because that's exactly what I've just told them they should look at."

Suicide hadn't crossed Marjorie's mind, which was rather remiss of her, but the thought that Dolores Hagman might have taken her own life didn't fit with what she'd witnessed on the first day of the holiday.

"I find that difficult to believe. The detective confirmed that Mrs Hagman had telephoned Philippa Trombone. Apparently, she told her friend she was in fear for her life."

"Is that what she said? Nothing surprises me when it comes to old Dolores. My guess is it was all part of an elaborate plan to sow seeds of doubt that would put us all under suspicion before she damn well killed herself. The woman was a drama queen, nothing more, nothing less. You must have recognised that, even in the brief space of time between you arriving at the hotel and our trip to the opera. Weren't you sat near her when she was doing all that blasted humming throughout the performance? Hardly normal behaviour, was it?"

"It's not unheard of for people to lose themselves in a performance. Isn't there a condition where people can become overwhelmed by artistic beauty?"

"Stendhal syndrome. But I hardly think that applies in this case. The performance was good, but it wasn't outstanding in any way."

"Perhaps it was to her," said Marjorie. "It might have brought back evocative memories of something in her past. Even if that weren't the case, beauty is very individual, as you well know, Major. What I think is wonderful, you might conclude is ordinary."

"You make a good point, but not in this case. I don't believe Dolores humming was anything to do with the Stendhal effect. She was attention seeking. Dolores was unhinged. She'd been acting weird for ages, ever since... well, you heard what happened with her ex."

A waiter approached the table and the major ordered a whisky. "Will you join me?" he asked.

"It's a little early for me, and I've drunk far too much coffee this morning, but you go ahead."

Once the whisky glass was in his hand, Major Jeffries took a large swig. "This stuff's better than those damn pills the pharmacy sold me yesterday. Now, where were we? Ah yes, the suicide. I'm sure that's what it was. With that silly woman's death, Chloe's sudden surge of ecstasy, Denise behaving like a prima donna, and Martha mollycoddling the two of them, I wonder how you women make it through the day."

Marjorie half smiled as visions of Percy's tantrums, the major's complaining, and Frederick's moroseness came to mind. "We do our best. So, from what you're saying, Chloe isn't upset about her mother's death."

Major Jeffries cleared his throat, somewhat embarrassed. "I wouldn't go that far, but her mother was a tyrant. All the time I've known the daughter, she's been a timid little thing, frightened to speak because every word that came out of her mouth was criticised or belittled. I think the girl's like an uncoiled spring – gone a bit over the top, if you're an outsider looking in, but we understand why her behaviour's a bit, erm... wild."

"I see," said Marjorie, who didn't really see at all. From where she was sitting, the woman didn't give a fig about her mother, which begged the question: did she kill her? "Does Chloe Hagman work?"

"Not really, never been allowed to. Permanent companion-cum-dogsbody to her mother. I think Denise said she used to work, but she can't remember what it was she did. Nothing important."

"She wasn't on the stage, then?"

Major Jeffries guffawed. "Not likely. As I said before, she's always been under the screw. To be honest, I don't think her mother's death has sunk in yet."

"It sounds as though you may have known Dolores Hagman more than you let on, Major."

He cleared his throat again. "Perhaps I did, but we don't need to go into things like that. Hardly relevant. I will say again, though, the woman hasn't been happy of late. Mark my words, she took her own life."

"You say your daughter's behaving like a prima donna. Why do you think that is?"

"I'm not entirely sure. I tend not to get involved when she's like this. She'll soon snap out of it. We had her late in life, my wife was five years older than me. She's been spoilt rotten, but still —" Major Jeffries drained the rest of his whisky. "I'd better get back to the crew. It's been a pleasant respite speaking with you, Lady Marjorie. Tell that Horace fellow I'm most impressed with his command of the lingo."

"I will, but I expect you'll get the opportunity to tell him yourself if you're sharing an overnight sleeper."

"It's a good job he and your other friend will be there, otherwise someone might find a certain Percy Gainsborough dead in his bed tomorrow morning." The major chuckled away to himself as he returned to his friends.

Chapter 15

Edna arrived shortly after the major left. She burst breathlessly into sight, carrying four shopping bags.

"Thank goodness, I caught you just in time. I'll take these upstairs, then we'll go for lunch. I'm starving."

One of Marjorie's pet dislikes was people saying they're starving when they've probably never felt real hunger in their lives, let alone known what it was like to starve. Edna had a habit of overusing the expression, but Marjorie hadn't pulled her up on it. It was one of the many irritating things her cousin-in-law said and did. Marjorie had to choose her battles carefully, otherwise – heaven forbid – she and Edna would compete with Percy and Major Jeffries in the argumentative category.

What an awful thought.

Edna returned within minutes, still breathless. They made their way into the main restaurant for lunch.

"Are we going to sit at a big table in case *they* come in?" Edna asked.

"I'd rather enjoy a quiet lunch, if you don't mind. How about a table for one?"

"Ha, ha, you're so not funny, Marge. I get you, though. There's a table for two. I'll ask the maître d' if we can take it."

Moments later, they were seated and, after ordering lunch, Edna subjected Marjorie to half an hour's detail about her shopping trip. Finally, Edna stopped talking and folded her arms, smirking.

"I told you, you should have come, though, didn't I?"

"From what you've described, it sounds more like a whirlwind than a stroll around the shops. I don't think I'd have been able to keep up, even with my stick." Marjorie grinned mischievously.

"That's not what I mean. Guess who I saw when I was out?"

"Someone famous, by the look on your face."

"No. Your boyfriend, Fred Mackworth. He didn't see me, but I watched him skulking around. He went to a chemist shop and a tobacconist."

"He's not my boyfriend, Edna, and his name's Frederick," Marjorie snapped. "I didn't realise there was a pharmacy in the shopping centre. I'm sure Horace sent Major Jeffries off in another direction yesterday."

"Maybe it wasn't there when he last visited. I think it's a few years since he came here."

Not wanting to get back on to the topic of Frederick, lest it lead to further friction, Marjorie said, "Speaking of Major Jeffries, we had quite a chat after the police interviewed him."

It did the trick. Edna stopped eating for a moment. Marjorie had no idea where her cousin-in-law put all the food she ordered, but having polished off a large chicken salad starter, she had consumed almost the entire contents of a rich beef dish while dipping bread into the sauce. Marjorie had to look away frequently lest it put her off her own lunch.

"What did he have to say? Did Horace grill him?"

"I don't think it's Horace's place to grill anybody. He's there to assist when the young police officer gets stuck. If it makes you feel better, the major did say Horace's Romanian impressed him."

"I'm impressed too. Who would have thought our show-off Horace would come up with the goods for once, rather than just talk about them?"

"I agree with you there," said Marjorie.

"Did the major give you anything that would help us with our case?"

Marjorie smiled, pleased Edna was fully committed to the investigation. "A few things, actually, but the most disturbing was something that hadn't crossed my mind."

"Now this I've got to hear," said Edna, gleefully.

"He believes Dolores Hagman killed herself."

Edna slapped her own head. "Of course! Why didn't we think of that?" For once, the question was genuine and not accusing. "But what about the phone call to this Philippa Trombone thingummy woman?"

"I put the same question to him, and he implied Dolores may have been getting back at them in some way. He believes she may have called her friend to cast suspicion on them so that it would look like murder. He made it sound like it was some sort of final 'up yours' type of thing."

"I'm surprised you even know such expressions, Marge. It don't sound right coming from your mouth."

"It's good to know I still retain a few elements of surprise. I suppose what he suggests is quite plausible, with her husband leaving her for a younger woman and publicly humiliating her in such a nasty way. The major said Dolores Hagman had been miserable for some time."

"From what I saw of the diva and after hearing what she did to Fred, I doubt what her husband did was any more than she deserved. Although, if she did top herself and wanted one of her friends or family to be convicted of murder, that's just plain evil. Did he say where the money came from?"

"We didn't get on to that subject. I don't believe he would know anyway, but he let slip – or rather, I got the impression – he and Dolores had a relationship in the past."

"So much for not knowing her very well, eh? Naughty Major Jeffries. No wonder the husband ran out on her. I can't feel sorry for the woman.

Marge, although it's an awful thing to be driven to suicide."

"If it was suicide," said Marjorie. "I'm yet to be convinced. The only other useful information I got out of him was that his daughter and Chloe Hagman are behaving strangely; bizarrely, almost."

"You mean stranger than usual? They're an odd pair, that's for sure. I've noticed Chloe Hagman going around looking high as a kite since that night, after the initial shock. She's a weird woman anyway; probably takes after her mother. It wouldn't surprise me if she was on drugs. Either that or mental health problems run in the family, what with Martha and all."

"I hope she's not taking drugs. From what the major was saying about her mother's treatment of her, it sounds more like she's just pleased to have had a blessed release."

"Maybe Chloe put the cyanide in the flask. She would have had every opportunity."

Marjorie shook her head. "I don't see it being her. Chloe would have been too terrified of failure, and I have detected no malice in her during our brief encounters, unlike the rest of the group."

"Martha seems all right, considering she's been the ugly sister for all these years. I didn't take to her at first, but she must be a saint to put up with that husband of hers, not to mention the diva."

"Mm, I haven't worked Martha out yet, but she seems a kind sort and dotes on Chloe."

"The child she never had. I get that," Edna said, wistfully.

"The woman's hardly a child."

"Maybe not, but she behaves like one. Denise Jeffries is a peculiar sort, ain't she? One minute the caring, almost controlling daughter, and the next, Little Miss Angry. I wouldn't like to be on the wrong side of her."

"The major did admit she was behaving like a prima donna, although he implied this could be normal for her and suggested it would run its course. From what he says, he and his wife spoiled her and didn't rein her in."

"They're a rum lot, that's for sure, but it doesn't make any of them a murderer. I've got an inkling the major could be right and the woman on the slab is looking down, laughing at the chaos she's left behind."

"I can't believe anyone would be so cruel. And if she was that cruel, I doubt she'll be looking down at all. If a person is suicidal, how would they have the wherewithal to create such a web of confusion for after they have departed? Besides, from what Philippa Trombone told me, Dolores sounded frightened the night she phoned."

"You're forgetting, Marjorie, Dolores Hagman was an actress. This was her final curtain call and maybe, just maybe, she was determined to deliver the performance of her life. It would also explain why there was no suicide note. In order to kill her, someone would have had to know she had a flask and that she would take it with her to the opera, and they would also have to get it and add the poison. You say you're convinced Chloe didn't do it, so maybe no-one did."

"I'm certain the entire Hagman crew would know of the flask if she did indeed take it everywhere with her."

Edna was no longer listening. She wiped her mouth with a napkin.

"I'd take my hat off to Dolores the diva if she hadn't been so horrible."

"And if you had a hat," said Marjorie.

Was a dastardly plot really being orchestrated by a dead woman? And if so, was Philippa Trombone aware of it? Marjorie intended to find out.

Chapter 16

Having returned to her people-watching place off the lobby after lunch, Marjorie observed the remnants of the Hagman group. Edna had returned to her room to sort through her shopping and, no doubt, try on the new wig. The interviews seemed to be taking an eternity, considering there were only two that had carried over to the afternoon, as far as she could tell.

Frederick had given her a cursory nod on his return to the hotel. He didn't appear to be carrying any shopping bags, unlike Edna and the pile she had returned with. Marjorie felt it best to leave him to his own thoughts and not to pry, although she would have loved to find out what it was about him that gave him such an air of mystery.

He's secretive, she concluded.

Other hotel guests came and went throughout the afternoon, some leaving with bags and others arriving. It was interesting watching people viewing the opulent entrance and large lobby for the first time. Marjorie herself was impressed with how beautifully modern the area was, such a contrast to other parts of the city. The service, too, was commendable, with one waiter in particular standing out. Nelu, a man in his late twenties appeared to be trapped in a long battle with acne, but he didn't let it deter him. He made sure he was noticed without being obvious about it. Marjorie liked that he was clearly ambitious. He also remembered her name, another thing she liked.

"Can I get you more coffee, Lady Snellthorpe?"

"I don't think so. I've had more than I would usually drink. No offence, but I prefer tea. I just can't take to the tea the hotel serves."

“I have just the thing,” Nelu said, tapping his nose. “I’ll speak to Josie. She’s over here from England, taking a gap year, and I know she has a secret stock of English Breakfast teabags.”

Marjorie perked up. “Oh, if you could get something like that, I’d really appreciate it. Thank you, Nelu. If your friend doesn’t mind giving you a couple, I’m happy to pay her.”

“She won’t mind at all.”

Marjorie had a thought. “Nelu?”

“Yes, ma’am.”

“I don’t like to ask, but I wonder... No. Perhaps I should forget about it—”

“What is it, ma’am?”

“It might appear trivial in the grand scheme of things, but on the day I arrived, I loaned Mrs Hagman – the lady who unfortunately passed away – a booklet. I wouldn’t usually worry about such a thing, but my late husband gave it to me and I would like it back.”

"I could ask the inspector if he's seen it. What's the name of the book?"

"It's an original work called *The Hound of Heaven*. Mrs Hagman showed such an interest that I let her borrow it. She was going to give it back to me the next morning." Marjorie could imagine Edna's voice calling her Pinocchio, but she had gone too far to stop now. "I wouldn't want to trouble the inspector, and to be honest, I feel mean even asking about a booklet when a woman has lost her life. Do you know where they put her belongings?"

"As far as I know, they are still in her room. The inspector hasn't released her possessions yet, just in case. But Maria – she's the one taking drinks in and out of the Picasso Room – says she overheard them talking about suicide. So sad, she was a beautiful singer. She gave me a CD when I took drinks to her room."

"Oh, that is sad. But in that case, if her belongings are not being treated as part of a crime, do you think I might take a little peek? No-one needs to know but us."

Nelu sucked his lips, weighing up what to do. He glanced over to where the Hagman party were now indulging in alcoholic beverages.

“I tell you what. I’ll get you the pot of tea, and when I return, you can ask for me to bring it up to your room. You’re only a few doors down from where Dolores… erm… Mrs Hagman was staying.”

“I wouldn’t want you to get into trouble,” Marjorie said, having second thoughts.

“As you say, the book has personal value to you. It should be all right.”

Marjorie remained seated, her heart pounding for the ten minutes it took for Nelu to track down his friend and return with her tea. She hoped her beloved English tea wouldn’t go cold during the risky endeavour she was about to undertake. Her heart had missed a beat when she saw Chloe get up, but she had been relieved to see her walking unsteadily to and from the ladies.

“Tea, ma’am,” Nelu said loudly, making a good pretence of being about to place it on the table.

Marjorie looked up at him, conveniently just as Martha Gainsborough was returning from the interview room.

“Actually, would you mind bringing it up to my room, Nelu? I’m getting rather stiff sitting here.”

“Of course, Lady Snellthorpe. My pleasure.”

They took the lift together up to her floor and, after making sure the corridor was clear, Nelu walked past her room to another one, four doors down. He knocked before sliding his universal pass to open the door. He held the tea tray in one hand and pushed the door open for Marjorie with the other.

“It will be better if I don’t come in. I’ll take the tea to your room, and then hang around in the corridor. I’ve asked Josie to let me know if any of the family or friends move. She was just going on duty when I got the tea, and lucky for us, she works behind the bar.”

"Thank you, Nelu. I'll be as quick as I can."

Once the door closed, Marjorie felt a sense of nervous excitement. Even if she was to be discovered, she could relate the story of the booklet again. She did love the precious first edition of Francis Thompson's epic poem her husband had given her, but would never have loaned it to anyone, especially not Dolores Hagman. It was far too fragile these days and she kept it in a plastic bag inside her handbag. Even when reading it, she had to be careful.

As she grasped the handle of the first drawer, the opening lines came to mind:

I fled Him, down the nights and down the days;
I fled Him, down the arches of the years;
I fled Him, down the labyrinthine ways
Of my own mind; and in the midst of tears
I hid from Him, and under running laughter.
Up vistaed hopes, I sped;
And shot, precipitated,
Adown Titanic glooms of chasmèd fears,

From those strong Feet that followed, followed after.

But with unhurrying chase,
And unperturbèd pace,
Deliberate speed, majestic instancy,
They beat—and a Voice beat
More instant than the feet—
"All things betray thee, who betrayest Me."

Marjorie shuddered, remembering the moral of the lengthy poem was that a loving God would pursue the evil doer to bring him to repentance. Guilt pangs caused her to hesitate. But when she reminded herself that her presence was all about getting justice for a murdered woman, she felt the good Lord would approve of the outcome, if not the process.

She opened and closed drawers and suitcases. From the amount of luggage in the room, she suspected Dolores had packed as if she would be away for three months rather than two weeks. Marjorie was hoping to find a diary or some other clues as to Dolores's state of mind, but she wasn't having much success. She checked all the places where she herself hid things when staying in a hotel – under the mattress, under the pillows, inside Dolores's shoes and stockings – but there was nothing to be found.

She studied Dolores Hagman's passport, which she had found in the top drawer of the bedside table.

"Dear me, fancy leaving a passport out in the open like that."

Marjorie checked the photograph and flicked through the pages. There was nothing other than an open US visa. Returning to the photograph page, she took the passport to the wardrobe and found the safe in the same place as the one in her own room.

"I wonder," she muttered before using a combination of numbers from the date of birth. Voila! The safe clicked open. This made Dolores's faux pas of leaving her passport in a drawer even more remiss.

Inside the safe, Marjorie fingered through the usual items such as cash, jewellery, house keys and the like. She moved things around and pulled out a letter from underneath a cardboard folder containing euros. Marjorie opened the letter, which she hoped might contain important information. Instead, it was a letter from a literary agent congratulating Dolores Hagman on a book and film deal.

A knock at the door drew her attention away from its contents and she returned it, popping the passport in the safe too before closing it just as Nelu poked his head around the door.

“Miss Hagman is on her way upstairs.” His voice cracked with stress.

“I’ll be right there. I found what I was looking for.” Marjorie took the precious booklet from her handbag and showed it to him.

“Very good, ma’am. Come quickly.”

Marjorie and Nelu entered her room just as she heard the lift door ping as it stopped on the same floor. Once inside, she reached into her handbag and gave him a large tip.

"The booklet is so precious to me, I can't thank you enough."

Nelu's brown eyes widened as he looked at the money in his hand. "That's too much, Lady Marjorie. I don't think I can take it."

"Tosh. You've been extremely helpful. Give your friend Josie some of it if it makes you feel better."

Nelu grinned. "Thank you, I will." He tucked the notes in his pocket.

"I think you're sweet on her."

"I do like her, but not in that way. She's like a younger sister. I like to look out for her. Not everyone in Romania is honest and I have sisters at home. I'd like to think someone would do the same for them if they were away."

Marjorie liked this young man even more. He was definitely ambitious, but not callous. There was an honesty and guileless innocence about him which she hoped would remain.

"I'm going to enjoy this wonderful English tea now. Thank you for your help, Nelu."

“You’re most welcome. Sorry the tea might be cold, but I’ve left you some teabags on the tray.”

“Wonderful, and I shall enjoy this tea, anyway.”

After Nelu left her to her lukewarm tea, Marjorie pondered for a while. Her foray into Dolores Hagman’s room had given her a little more information than she already had, but nothing leapt out at her. The only odd thing was the amount of clothes the woman had packed, but that fact might not be significant, unless...

Marjorie poured herself another cup of tea. “Unless she was running away.”

Chapter 17

Over dinner, Horace was reticent to reveal any details of his time in the interview room while Frederick was sitting at their table. The latter appeared to have put the matter of Dolores Hagman's untimely demise out of his head as the rather strong wine loosened his tongue. It became perfectly clear he wasn't used to alcohol, other than the odd drop of brandy. Tonight he was the most animated Marjorie had seen him since they met.

"I saw you in the shopping centre today. What were you buying?" Edna, never one to hold back, asked; or rather, demanded. A subtle circle of pink appeared on Frederick's cheeks and on the top of his bald head, making it shimmer.

"Just a few items for my nephew."

"Cigars or cigarettes?" Edna wouldn't let up once she started.

"Tobacco actually. I don't smoke myself, but he smokes a pipe. He asked me to pick up some Romanian tobacco."

"There aren't many pipe smokers around these days," said Horace. "Especially not among the younger generations."

Frederick laughed. "My nephew's older than me. I was what you might call a surprise. My parents thought they were long past it—"

"When out you popped." Edna snorted and Horace guffawed.

"Something like that. Changing the subject, how's our investigation going? I rather got the impression from Simon the police now believe Dolores committed suicide."

"First-name terms with the major now, are we?" said Edna.

Frederick ignored the barb and Horace shuffled in his seat, looking thoughtful before answering. "That's one line of enquiry. I'm not allowed to discuss the case with anyone. The inspector made it quite clear he wouldn't be happy if I divulged any information from the interviews."

"But surely you can tell us... after all, we're carrying out our own investigation, aren't we?"

"I haven't seen you doing anything to help so far. Your absence has been noted." Edna narrowed her eyes, staring at Frederick.

"Well, I, erm—"

"Leave the man alone, Edna," said Marjorie. Turning to Frederick, she smiled in what she hoped was a kind way. "We thought it would be better to leave any investigating to the police. After all, it's nothing to do with us. We didn't know Dolores Hagman and we don't really want to get to know her friends and relatives any more than we have to."

Fredrick stared into his wineglass. She detected a tear in the confused man's eyes. He tried to speak, but either the drink or the emotion got the better of him. Instead, he plonked the wineglass on the table and pushed his chair back.

"I'm going to pack. I'll see you on the train." With that, he tried to leave with head held high, but failed miserably, swaying across the floor as he exited the dining room.

"Methinks someone's a tad squiffy," mocked Edna.

"I feel a bit bad not letting him in on the act, but unfortunately, he could be the prime suspect," Horace declared. "Every one of the Hagman party elaborated on how he had vowed to get his own back after being dumped on his wedding day. Yelled it out loud in the church in front of over a hundred witnesses."

"Martha said she'd never met Fred before," said Edna.

"You're right. In fact, none of them were invited to the wedding, and Chloe and Denise hadn't even been born then, but the story's been handed down over the years."

"So, none of them actually witnessed this so-called threat. Besides, that was decades ago,' said Marjorie. "Surely they can't believe threats made in a man's younger days count now?"

"Watch what you say, Horace. She's soft on him," said Edna, winking.

"Grow up, Edna. This is serious business. We can't see a man arrested for a murder he didn't commit."

Horace cleared his throat, looking increasingly uncomfortable. "I, erm—"

"What is it?" Marjorie snapped.

"I'm afraid our Frederick has been holding back on us. A waitress saw him go inside the late woman's room on the afternoon of the opera, not long after we went upstairs following the fractious lunch. Also, the people in the room next door to her – a French couple, who are not connected to the Hagman party – heard loud voices around the same time. Well, mostly one loud voice: that of a woman, presumably Dolores. They were about to call reception to complain when they heard her yell at her companion – presumably Fred – to get out. After that, they heard the door open and close and that was the end of it."

"It might just mean he was too embarrassed to tell us she rejected him again," said Edna, looking at Marjorie with sympathy.

"While the argument was going on, the couple heard one of the people entering the bathroom and water running. As Inspector Radu points out, that gives Fred ample time to put cyanide in her flask."

"Which he just happens to be carrying in his pocket," said Marjorie, exasperated. "Did this couple with the unusually acute hearing tell of any other comings and goings, by any chance?"

"I'm afraid the police didn't ask them. I wanted to ask, but Inspector Radu dismissed them. After their statement, he seemed set on it being our Fred, I'm afraid."

"What excuse did Frederick have for all of this?" Marjorie asked.

"At first, he went quiet, then flatly denied being in her room."

"And what did he say about the waitress's statement?" Marjorie was struggling between feeling angry at Frederick and let down, but she still couldn't believe he was a cold-blooded murderer.

"He said the woman was mistaken."

"He's hardly unrecognisable with that shiny head, is he?" Edna chortled.

"That point was put to him, in a slightly less offensive fashion, but he maintains he never went inside the room."

"So, did the police re-question the waitress?"

"No. She'd gone home by the time we interviewed Fred. He was the last to turn up. The staff had trouble tracking him down."

“Because he was out shopping,” said Edna, “buying tobacco for his older nephew and a side-order of cyanide from the chemist.”

“Oh, do be serious, Edna,” snapped Marjorie.

“The good news for Fred is that whilst the inspector was, and might still be, heading in his direction, he has thrown him a lifeline. Major Jeffries postulated the idea of Dolores taking her own life. Fred’s right about that being seriously considered as one line of enquiry.”

“I expect that’s why Frederick was asking about that tonight,” said Marjorie. “Major Jeffries said the same thing to me. Edna and I discussed his theory over lunch.”

“I agree with you, though, Marjorie. I can’t see Fred, or any sane person, bearing a grudge so deep for all these years, and then killing the woman as soon as he meets her again. Especially not in the light of his being happily married for decades. He’s not done himself any favours denying being in the room when he was seen, mind.”

"Agreed," said Marjorie. "That was rather foolish."

"So, the inspector is taking the suicide theory seriously, then?" Edna quizzed.

"He pooh-poohed it at first, but when I pointed out to him that several interviewees had mentioned her mental state, he admitted it might be more plausible than a man she's not seen in over forty years turning up out of the blue and poisoning her."

A horrid thought crossed Marjorie's mind. "You don't think he knew she would be here, do you?"

"I can't see how. It genuinely shocked him when he first saw her," said Edna. "Even I noticed how white he went."

Marjorie exhaled, relieved. "Then it must be one of the others who killed her. I'm not convinced by this suicide nonsense. I believe she was running away from something."

"What makes you say that?" asked Horace.

Marjorie explained about her subterfuge after Edna had left her this afternoon, how she'd persuaded Nelu to let her inside Dolores Hagman's room.

"You should have told me, Marge. Someone might have seen you."

"Edna's right," said Horace. "If there is a killer among us, we don't want you being put at risk. I remember what happened the last time."

Marjorie also remembered how, if Edna hadn't turned up just in time on their previous holiday, she might have been killed.

"Nelu was keeping an eye out for me and he had a spy downstairs watching the Hagman party's every move."

"How do you know you can trust this Nelu? He might sell the information."

"That's preposterous. He's a kind young man. Besides, he believed my story and I showed him the booklet. I always have it with me, so what is there to tell?"

"You still haven't said why you think she was running away," said Edna.

"She had far too many suitcases to be travelling on a two-week voyage."

"Maybe she liked to carry an assortment of clothes. She could obviously afford it," argued Edna.

Marjorie shook her head. The more she thought about the suitcases, the passport, and the letter from the agent, the more she believed Dolores had been leaving for good.

"I didn't have time to go through the contents of her safe properly, but there was a letter from a literary agent in America congratulating her on a book deal. She also had an open visa for the United States in her passport, so I believe she was planning on going there. I expect if I'd have had more time, I would have found an airline ticket."

"That's rather a leap of the imagination, isn't it?" said Horace. "If she was going anywhere, why the States? An open visa and a letter from America don't confirm she was heading there.

And why now? And why didn't she tell her best friend?"

Marjorie felt deflated. "I don't have all the answers, and I don't understand why she wouldn't have told Miss Trombone. Perhaps she didn't trust anyone with her plan, or maybe her friend knew and was sworn to secrecy."

"Except there would be no need to keep it a secret after she turned up dead, would there?" Edna stated.

"Is it the presence of the suitcases that makes you believe someone murdered her rather than she committed suicide?" Horace asked.

"That, and the letter. Why would Dolores bring a letter from her agent on holiday with her unless she needed it? Oh, I do wish Nelu hadn't interrupted me when he did. I don't suppose we could get into her room again?" Marjorie looked hopefully towards Horace.

"I'm afraid not. The room's being cleared as we speak. I don't know whether the police are keeping her stuff here or sending it back to the UK."

"The former, I would imagine, at least for now," Marjorie said.

"What if Major Jeffries is right, though, Marge? What if Dolores killed herself, and before she did the deed, she persuaded this Philippa Trombone woman to create havoc after she was gone? Obviously, she wasn't to know her old fiancé would become a prime suspect. I expect she was hoping to put one of that motley crew in the frame for murder."

"But why? I can't say I took to Dolores from the little I saw of her and knowing what she did to Frederick all those years ago, but to implicate your friends and family in a false crime is – as you said earlier – just evil."

"Some people are that bad. Plain and simple," said Horace. "Human nature's a funny thing. Maybe she was born with a devil's gene."

"I don't believe people are born evil," said Marjorie. "Something makes them that way or they choose to follow a dark path for some other reason."

"Opera is full of dark and twisted souls. Perhaps she was too immature, even at her age, to distinguish between fact and fiction."

"And now she's playing out her own opera from the grave – well, from the morgue at least," said Edna.

Marjorie felt herself frown. "No, I don't accept that. I have no doubt Dolores Hagman was murdered."

Chapter 18

Marjorie would be pleased to get inside the train station. Having to endure endless arguing between Percy and Denise was grating on her nerves. She couldn't quite catch what they were arguing about, but it sounded like Percy was defending his long-time friend, Major Jeffries, from the sharp end of Denise's tongue. Frederick had sat alone on a back seat, still sulking, and Edna sat next to Horace, so Marjorie found herself sitting beside the major, with his daughter and Chloe in the seats behind. Percy and Martha were on the opposite side to them.

"I must apologise for my daughter, Lady Marjorie. As I said before, she's been badly affected by all of this suspicious death nonsense."

"Do call me Marjorie, please. And you don't need to apologise for your daughter, she's a grown woman." *Who should be the one apologising for her own behaviour*, remained unsaid. "Was your daughter close to Dolores?"

"Not at all, detested the woman. It's the inconvenience she's annoyed about. Denise doesn't like change and lives a very ordered life." He pinched his nose before lowering his voice. "Although, if you ask me, I think she's frightened."

"Frightened of what?"

"That one of our gang might turn out to be a murderer. Preposterous, I know, but Denise always had a vivid imagination. Suffered terrible nightmares as a child. We overindulged her, partly because of the nightmares, partly with being parents later in life and because she was an only child. Trouble is, now she believes she can talk to anyone how she pleases. I don't take too much notice, but it doesn't always make her popular, especially with the opposite sex, if you know what I mean."

"Some men don't like opinionated women, granted, but that shouldn't be the case in this day and age. Has Denise ever been married?"

"She was engaged once, but the fella broke it off. They lived together for five years. I guess that was enough to put him off," the major shrugged his shoulders. "Problem is, she's a chip off the old block. You might not believe it, but I wasn't easy to live with."

Marjorie felt it best not to respond to that remark, asking instead, "Are you still convinced Dolores Hagman's death was suicide?"

"Quite certain of it. I've tried to tell Denise the same thing, but she's been snappy all day as you can hear—"

Marjorie could certainly hear Denise and Percy arguing, as could everybody else on the minibus.

"She didn't see why she had to be interviewed 'like a criminal', as she put it, and now she's convinced she knows who the killer is."

"Really? Who? Perhaps she should tell the police." Marjorie's interest was piqued.

The major pinched his nose again. "Better not say, don't want to start rumours. Besides, it's stuff and nonsense. Dolores was trouble in life, now she's being trouble in death. If I'm honest, Lady... sorry, erm... Marjorie, I regret coming away. Blasted hip's given me nothing but gip; I dread to think what it will be like after a night of being thrown about on a rattling old train."

"I believe Romania has some newer trains. Let's hope we get one of those, although I do sympathise. Long train journeys aren't the best as one gets older. Although I'd make an exception to try the Orient Express." Marjorie wasn't exactly looking forward to the night ahead of her, either. Sharing a sleeper with Edna had to be some sort of purgatory.

"There's the station, Marge." As if by magic, Edna's voice reminded her of what was to come. Marjorie peered out of the window and was pleased to see a building sympathetically made up of the old and the new.

“After the opera the other night, I’d expected it to look older, or more rundown,” she remarked.

“Faith was telling me earlier it’s been fully modernised,” said the major. Perhaps they would get a modern train after all.

Alas, once they were through the beautiful arched entrance and inside a very modern-looking railway station, Marjorie’s hopes were shattered. The overnight train was one of the older stock.

“Blimey, I thought we would at least get a luxury train for the inconvenience of not flying. I mean, it’s not our fault Dolores Hagman topped herself, is it?” Edna complained.

“Or was murdered,” said Marjorie. “We must keep an open mind, remember?”

“Is that it?” Both women turned on hearing Denise Jeffries yelling again. Her latest ire was aimed in Faith’s direction.

“I’m told the sleeping compartments are comfortable,” said Faith.

“They’d better be,” Percy piped up, adversary now turned advocate. “If I’ve got to share with three other men, I’m going to need no less than five-star accommodation.”

“Good luck with that.” Edna laughed, nudging Marjorie. Thankfully, Percy didn’t hear. “Did you hear those two bickering all the way here? Now look at them behaving like they’re best mates. I’ll be glad to see the back of them all when we get to Bucharest.”

“But we need to stay in touch with them if we’re going to find out what happened to Dolores,” said Marjorie.

“You can do what you like, but I’ve had my fill of ’em, Marge. I’m likely to punch that Percy on the nose if I have to listen to his snotty voice much longer, and as for that spoilt brat, Denise… I don’t know how Martha puts up with Percy Snooty GainsBellows. Mouth like a foghorn. He’s got to be the most obnoxious man I've ever had the displeasure to meet, and I've met some in my time."

"Please hush, Edna. Someone will hear you." Marjorie took the other woman's arm and led her away from the disgruntled group gathering around Faith. Horace joined them.

"Poor Faith. I hope she's being paid a lot of money because she's going to earn every penny of it," he said, shaking his head.

"I don't see the point of complaining," said Marjorie. "Surely they can't expect her to magic up a train from nowhere. Besides, it's not brand new, but I'm sure it will be perfectly adequate. It's not as if we're going to have to sit up all night, is it?"

"Speak for yourself. I don't think I'll get a wink in a compartment with those three."

"Fred will be all right. Look at him, he's not said a word."

Their eyes followed Edna's to a forlorn-looking Frederick leaning against a wall. "Should I cheer the chap up?" Horace asked.

“No, I think you had better rescue Faith. I believe Denise Jeffries is losing control.”

Denise’s shouting was verging on hysteria, and the others weren’t helping with their complaining. But before Horace could move, Frederick shocked them all by yelling.

“STOP IT! JUST STOP SHOUTING, WILL YOU?”

It worked. The Hagman party backed off from Faith and muttered amongst themselves for a while. Just long enough for Faith to regain control and call them all together as a large group.

“We have forty minutes before the train leaves. As you can see, there are many shops open where you can buy drinks, pastries and cakes, or you can board the train and get settled in. I prearranged for the porter to store your luggage in the baggage compartment once you’ve taken what you need for the night. That should give you extra space. There’s a first-class dining car on board if you can’t sleep, which sells food, soft drinks and alcohol. Please be considerate to your sleeping companions and try not to disturb them during the night if you can."

"Fat chance of that with my prostate," said Major Jeffries. Percy opened his mouth to say something sarcastic, but following a nudge from his wife, he settled for an eye roll.

Horace rubbed his hands together. "Let the fun commence."

"Before you go off and spend the night with your new bed mates—"

"Steady on!" said Horace.

"You know what I mean. Anyway, before you go, I need you, or rather your Romanian, to help me buy a few cream cakes for the journey," said Edna. "Do you want anything, Marge?"

Just a new holiday companion, but Marjorie replied, "No, thank you. I wouldn't want the sugar keeping me awake." *Your snoring will be quite enough,* also remained unsaid.

"Suit yourself. I won't have any trouble sleeping. I've got some pills the doctor gave me after my Dennis died."

Bully for you, thought Marjorie, saying, "I'll wait here for you. It's a warm evening."

While Horace and Edna went off in pursuit of confectionary, Marjorie sat on a railway bench in the centre of the platform. She heard various announcements filtering through the station, all in Romanian. She caught the names of destinations she had heard of, such as Oradea, which she believed was close to the Hungarian border, and even *Budapesti* itself, the latter being their final destination if they ever got on the Danube river cruise.

Marjorie inhaled and exhaled deep and slow breaths, trying to prepare herself for the night ahead. She watched people boarding the train, most chatting excitedly, a few families leading tired-looking children and one couple arguing. Most of the people she observed were Romanian, but she also heard several tourists speaking German and a group of teenagers speaking French. Probably a school trip.

While Marjorie was watching the French party, her attention was drawn to the far end of the platform on hearing the sharp voice of an Englishwoman. The voice, which was berating a porter for mishandling its owner's luggage, had a familiar ring, but Marjorie couldn't make out who she was. The woman was too far away and the porter blocked her view.

"Sorry about shouting like that."

Marjorie had felt someone take a seat on the bench while straining her eyes to catch a glimpse of the Englishwoman, so she hadn't looked to see who it was. Frederick was wringing his hands again.

"I don't blame you for not wanting to speak to me."

"Pardon? No, it's not that. I was miles away, watching the comings and goings of people boarding the train. Train stations the world over are such interesting places, aren't they? All manner of people travelling to destinations unknown, I get lost in my own thoughts sometimes. You're quite wrong about my not wanting to speak to you. And if you're referring to your timely intervention with Faith, you did the right thing. Horace was about to do as much himself. It really wasn't fair, them ganging up on her like that."

"Still friends, then? I feel like the three of you have been avoiding me."

"Not at all. We just wanted to give you some space, that's all. You've had quite a shock."

"Dolores, you mean? The thing is, it really was a very long time ago. Of course, I wanted to find out why she did what she did. I thought perhaps the years might have mellowed her, you know, but the way I see it now, I had a lucky escape. My late wife, Flora..."

Marjorie had to suppress a smile. Frederick and Flora sounded like it should be the name of a TV show.

"...was a wonderful woman. We never shared the, erm, same passion as Dolores and I did, but our relationship went deeper than that."

Marjorie hoped Frederick would not share any details of his sex life and was pleased when he moved on.

"I have two boys and a daughter. I wouldn't want to turn the clock back, not for one minute. Do you have any children?"

"I have a son. He runs the business my late husband built from scratch."

"Are you close?"

"Not as close as I'd like, but we love each other and that's the most important thing, I feel."

Marjorie wanted to believe Frederick wasn't involved in Dolores Hagman's death and what he was saying was true, but there was the question of his being seen entering her room on the day of the opera, and then being heard arguing with her. Until ten minutes ago, Marjorie had felt the mild-mannered Frederick Mackworth incapable of raising his voice, but having witnessed his outburst, albeit in a worthy cause, her illusion had been shattered.

“Horace and Edna have gone to buy cake before boarding.”

“His Romanian is excellent. He obviously studied the language when he did business over here,” said Frederick, accepting the change of subject graciously.

Marjorie didn’t want to mention the Romanian blood because it wasn’t her story to tell, so she just nodded before adding, “Poor man’s been roped into continuing with his translation. Did you hear the inspector and the constable will join us in Bucharest?”

“Still? I’d hoped they would change their minds now they were leaning towards suicide. Having the police around is hardly conducive to a relaxing holiday.” Frederick frowned before getting up. “I’d better get on board. See you in Bucharest.”

“I hope you get some sleep,” Marjorie offered, but Frederick was gone. *What’s got into people? Where’s the common courtesy of yesterday?* Marjorie wondered now if Frederick had taken her for a fool in order to extract information about the investigation from her. She so wanted to trust him, but felt she needed to be a little more guarded around him.

Edna and Horace appeared in front of her.

"Come on, Marge. Time to get on with our journey."

"Journey indeed," she said, "but I wonder what malice awaits us."

"Chin up, Lady Marjorie. All will be well, you'll see," said Horace.

"Yeah, don't sound so maudlin. What's wrong, Marge?"

"Never mind me. There's nothing a good night's sleep won't cure."

Chapter 19

Marjorie tossed and turned, finding it impossible to sleep. The rhythmic sound of the train making its way through the Romanian countryside would have sent her off into a doze if it weren't for the regular jolts caused by it switching tracks. Then there was the snoring. How one person could make so much noise through their airways was a mystery. Edna's husband couldn't have got much sleep during their long marriage without earplugs, of that she was certain.

But rising above both of these issues, Marjorie found her mind preoccupied with the conundrum of who killed Dolores Hagman, coupled with the disappointment that Frederick might be taking advantage of her. It was no good. She would not get any rest while her mind was whirring. Perhaps a brandy would help.

Marjorie slipped on the dress she had hung at the end of the bed just in case, then she left her cousin-in-law booming unpleasant sounds at the walls of the rather confined sleeper. She had seen a car marked *Masina Bufet* on boarding the train, which Horace informed her translated as buffet car, so knew which direction to follow. A cabin door opened and she saw Chloe Hagman making her way along the corridor ahead of her. Marjorie was about to say hello, but the younger woman stopped to let herself into the toilet, locking the door behind her. Marjorie was passing from one carriage to the next when she found Martha gazing out of the train's window into the black night.

"I take it you can't sleep either," said Marjorie, making the other woman jump.

"I didn't hear you coming. You startled me. I never sleep well at this time of night; I'm a late-night person. It comes from working in the theatre for many years, I suspect. My sister was the same." The hint of a tear appeared in the corner of Martha's right eye, only just visible in the dimly lit corridor.

"It must be hard losing a sister. I expect you were close." If what Marjorie had heard already was true, it was the exact opposite.

"Not really. Dolores changed after she tasted fame and the high life. She became distant and full of herself, but as children, we were inseparable. I'm sorry to say that my sister hadn't turned in to a nice or a good person. But I still miss the person she once was."

"I expect her daughter misses her, too. How is she?"

"Bearing up. Actually, Chloe's doing better than bearing up. She seems almost relieved now she's rid of the responsibility. She and her mother had a tempestuous relationship. Dolores wasn't happy unless she was putting someone down, and these days, that tended to be Chloe. Percy was telling the truth when he said we only kept in touch because of Chloe."

"I see," said Marjorie. So far, Martha was being honest. "And what do you think of the major's theory that your sister committed suicide and engaged, or manipulated, her friend Philippa to cause trouble after her death?"

"He's got a vivid imagination, is what I think. He most likely wants to draw attention away from the ongoing dispute between Dolores and his daughter."

"Denise?"

"Yes, the one who's been shouting her mouth off all day. Methinks the lady protests too much, to coin a phrase."

"Are you suggesting Denise Jeffries may have had something to do with your sister's death?"

Martha stared into the black night once more. "I'm not sure, but they loathed each other."

"I hadn't picked that up, although I could tell Denise didn't care for her. 'Loathe' is a strong word. Do you have any idea why?" Marjorie asked.

"I'm not supposed to know, but Denise told Chloe, who told me: Dolores and Simon had a fling while Denise's mother was dying of cancer. That's the kind of woman my sister was: selfish and reckless. You already heard about how she dumped your boyfriend, Frederick Mackworth, at the altar."

"He's hardly my boyfriend. I don't know where you heard that, but it isn't true. We only just met."

"Funny him turning up out of the blue after all these years, don't you think?"

"I hadn't given it much thought," said Marjorie. The truth is, she had given it a lot of thought, but hadn't come to any conclusion.

"So there's two people with a motive for killing Dolores, for starters. Knowing my sister, I expect there's a long line of suspects for the police to sift through."

"But only six present on the night of the opera," said Marjorie.

Martha turned, looking Marjorie in the eyes. Her lips twitched and the mole on her chin appeared to wobble.

"You can't think anyone other than those I've mentioned had anything to do with it?"

"Luckily, I'm not the one paid to think. I'm just a tourist who's happy to leave that sort of thing to the police." At that moment, the carriages jarred as the train once more changed lines. Martha caught hold of Marjorie before she took a tumble. "Thank you. I'd better get on to the dining car before I end up on the floor. Goodnight, Martha."

The other woman turned away and went back to staring out of the window, no longer acknowledging Marjorie, who made her way unsteadily to the dining car. She arrived just in time to see Percy Gainsborough leaving. He nodded as he passed her, holding two takeaway cups, one most likely for his wife.

There were just a few people in the car and she asked the man behind the bar for a brandy. He didn't understand, so she pointed to the bottle. Marjorie sat alone for some time, mulling over the detail of the major's affair. He had virtually admitted to having a dalliance with the dead woman, but the timing of it would have been hard on Denise.

Having observed Denise's *Jekyll and Hyde* behaviour, she could well believe the woman capable of dropping poison into Dolores Hagman's drink. That said, it wouldn't be a stretch too far to imagine at least four of the five, not to mention Frederick, doing the same. Chloe's meek and mild drudge persona had totally transformed since her mother's death. Martha seemed an unlikely candidate, but openly admitted not liking her sister. Percy was angry enough with the world to be capable of anything. The least likely, in her opinion, was the major. Marjorie wondered if Martha's supposition was correct: that his suicide theory was a red herring designed to protect his daughter. He'd also told Marjorie on the bus that Denise thought she knew who the killer was, which could have been designed to throw her off the scent.

Marjorie took a sip of brandy and noticed Horace and Edna entering the buffet car.

“Thought I’d find you here, Marge. Do you want another one of those?”

Looking at her empty plastic cup, she nodded. “I wouldn’t mind a refill if you’re buying. I won’t take any more money from Horace until we’ve bought our share.”

“Fine,” Edna huffed. Horace, on pain of death, allowed Edna to pay, and then the two joined Marjorie at the table.

“I thought you took sleeping pills?” Marjorie said to Edna.

“I forgot. I’ve barely slept a wink.”

“You appeared to be sleeping soundly when I left. I’m surprised the whole corridor didn’t hear you. What time is it anyway?”

“Three-thirty,” said Horace after checking his watch. “Too stuffy in our cabin, not to mention it being like Paddington Station, with people in and out all the time. The only one still sleeping is the major, despite his prostate and hip problems. None of us got a wink until he and Percy stopped yapping at each other. Fred left first, scuttled out about midnight."

"Is he not back?" Marjorie couldn't hide the concern in her voice. She hadn't seen him.

"He got back as I was leaving. Said he'd been for a walk. We passed Percy on the way here."

"He left this carriage as I arrived," Marjorie said. "Was Martha with him? She was standing between the two carriages."

"No, she must have gone back to bed."

"I also saw Chloe go into a toilet, but she hasn't been this way," said Marjorie.

"Hardly worth the expense of sleeping carriages, is it?" Horace laughed, taking a swig of whisky. "Cheers."

"I had rather an interesting conversation with Martha on the way here." Marjorie explained what she had uncovered about the timing of

Major Jeffries's affair with Dolores and how Martha told her Denise hated the dead woman.

"I already said I wouldn't put it past her. She's a nasty piece of work, but why now?" Edna said.

"That's what's so frustrating about this case. Why are these people, who clearly have issues with each other, on this holiday at all?" Marjorie said. "One of them, if the major's theory is incorrect, came to commit murder, but they really are a loathsome group. I can't imagine why they bother with each other."

"Maybe Dolores got them all together to do the dirty on them like the major says," said Edna. "She could have blackmailed them into coming on the trip."

"That would be an excellent theory," Marjorie said, "except Philippa Trombone said Dolores hadn't been keen on the holiday, and had wanted her to come along. Plus, she called her on the night she died, saying she thought she had made a big mistake."

"Didn't someone say it was a double birthday celebration?" asked Horace. "I should have taken notes when we were interviewing, but I don't believe Inspector Radu would have been happy for me to do so."

"Perhaps we can get a copy from Danielle. She seems an amenable sort of person," suggested Marjorie. "But I remember it was Percy who told us about the birthday dos. He said Martha and the major share the same birthday, so they intended the holiday to be a joint celebration."

"I'm going back to bed. I'm sick of playing amateur detective," said Edna, getting up and heading back the way she had come.

"What's the matter with her?" asked Horace.

"Nothing much, except for not getting enough attention. Although, I fear she needs more sleep than the rest of us. I think it is time to turn in, though. If I hurry, I might get to sleep before the snoring starts." Marjorie chuckled.

"I'll stay for another nightcap. See you early in the morning. Goodnight, Marjorie."

"Goodnight. Give us a knock if we sleep in, won't you?"

Horace's laughter followed her out of the carriage. Time to rest the brain before the next leg of the journey.

"Have you seen Chloe?" Martha almost knocked Marjorie over as she switched carriages.

Horace appeared behind Marjorie. She guessed he must have heard the commotion.

"What's the matter?"

"Chloe. Have you seen Chloe? She's not in our compartment."

"I saw her going into the toilet, but that was hours ago, before I bumped into you," said Marjorie.

"Which toilet? Where?" Martha snatched at Marjorie's wrist.

"The one at the end of our corridor."

"Perhaps she's fainted or found a better place to sleep." Horace's attempt to make light of the situation fell on deaf ears.

"I must find her. I do hope she hasn't done anything stupid." Martha turned and ran back towards their carriage. Horace and Marjorie exchanged a glance before following the crazed woman.

The toilet was unoccupied, although the window was open. Martha let out a cry and ran along the corridor, banging on the men's sleeper door.

Percy emerged first. "What the devil? Oh, it's you, Martha. What's the matter?"

Murmurings of complaint came from inside the men's cabin, soon followed by Edna and Marjorie's door being flung open.

"Keep it down, will you? I'm trying to sleep." Edna yelled.

Then, Faith came out of her room.

"That's the lot of us, then. So much for getting some sleep," said Horace.

"At least the toilet window's too small for her to have jumped, if that's what Martha was referring to when she said she hoped Chloe had done nothing stupid," Marjorie whispered to Horace. Then she asked, "Where's Denise? I don't see her here."

Horace shrugged his shoulders as Martha told the disgruntled group of people that Chloe was missing.

"I'm sure she's just gone for a hot chocolate or something. She'll be in the dining car," said the major, rubbing his hip. "Now if you'll excuse me, I need to use the facilities." He walked away from the gathered crowd to the opposite end of the carriage.

Martha's eyes widened. "She's not in the dining car. I've looked."

"She's right," said Horace, "unless there's another one. We've just come from the dining car ourselves."

"The buffet carriage in the direction you've come from separates standard from first-class passengers. There's another one for first class. The one you should have been using," Faith explained. "First-class dining is that way." She pointed in the direction the major had taken.

“Now she tells us,” complained Edna.

“I’m sure the brandy tastes the same in both carriages,” said Marjorie sarcastically.

“It’s all in the information that came with our tickets,” said Frederick. “I was there earlier.”

Chapter 20

Marjorie followed the crowd. Martha barged past Frederick, shoving him out of the way before heading towards the dining car that until moments ago, very few of them had been aware of.

"Slow down, Martha, she'll be in there." Percy's plea was ignored and they continued at speed, going against the direction of the train's travel.

"I hope nothing's happened to the poor woman. She seemed quite low earlier," said Faith, bringing up the rear with Marjorie. "I think the loss of her mother was finally sinking in."

Hanging back, Marjorie couldn't help feeling the next part of someone's devious plan had been played out.

"I don't like this," she said, as Edna and Horace slowed down to wait for them.

"What are you on about, Marge?"

"I have a sinking feeling that Chloe Hagman has followed her mother to the grave."

"They do say suicide runs in families," said Horace.

"Marge doesn't believe Dolores killed herself. So if she's right, neither has Chloe."

"Let's not get ahead of ourselves," said Horace. "This is likely nothing more than another case of insomnia, despite the hysteria. It's been like musical chairs all night."

They arrived in the dining car in time to witness Denise Jeffries being given the third degree by Martha Gainsborough.

"Where was she going?" the older woman screeched.

"How do I know? She didn't say, but she seemed agitated."

"What's happened?" Horace asked the major.

"Chloe left the sleeper in a huff when Denise turned the light on to read. Denise says she was annoyed Martha wasn't there. Apparently, Chloe told her she needed some space and left."

Marjorie shuffled past the maelstrom surrounding Denise with Edna seemingly glued to her back.

"Watch your step, Marge. I don't want you falling over."

The train had been lurching from side to side as if travelling over an uneven patch of track. Ignoring everyone else, Marjorie locked eyes with Denise.

"Have you seen Chloe since?"

"No." Denise shrugged her shoulders. "I thought she might be in here. I gave her long enough to get some space, but I got hungry."

Marjorie asked Horace to speak to the dining car manager and describe their missing companion. Horace did as requested and came back moments later.

“No help, I’m afraid. They changed shifts at the last stop. The woman who was on before him is now on a train heading back to Cluj. The only people he’s seen are Fred and Denise.”

Horace lowered his voice while the rest of the company continued their interrogations and accusations of who saw what, and when.

“He thinks he may have seen Martha in here and he definitely saw Percy.”

“Together?” asked Edna.

“No, separately. He can’t be certain about Martha, and it seems unlikely because she didn’t know about this car.”

“That’s odd because Percy was leaving the buffet car which we now know is in standard-class before you two arrived.”

“The only other thing the chap was able to tell me is: they all used the loo back that way.”

Horace indicated the opposite end of the carriage from where they had come in.

"Then I suggest we take a look. She certainly hasn't passed through the other buffet car. Maybe she used this dining carriage before the staff changeover. She might have gone for a walk or got stuck in the toilet."

"You're right. Perhaps she's taken ill," said Edna. "She looked a bit on the peaky side when I saw her back at the hotel."

The others were by now listening in to their conversation. This time, however, Marjorie led the throng at a more measured pace than previously, thankful that Edna stayed close, thereby preventing any of the others from overtaking. She stopped at the exit and allowed Edna to pull open the door so that she could step across the point where the two carriages joined.

Edna opened the second door and Marjorie passed through. Luggage blocked the sizeable gap between this and the next corridor. An extraneous noise was unmistakeable: bang,

bang, bang. A blast of air blew through a wide-open door, which was crashing against the side of the carriage. Marjorie felt the night's chill.

A scream pierced the air from the connecting corridor Marjorie had just left. Percy held on to Martha, who was nearing collapse.

Horace took charge.

"Stand back, everyone." Horace poked his head out of the train. Thankfully, it wasn't a super high-speed one. "Fred, Simon, hang on to me. I'm going to grab the door when it comes back this way."

The two men did as instructed. Once the opportunity arose, Horace pulled the door back in towards the train, forcing it closed against the opposing forces. With the door back where it should be, they could only hear the hum of the train, which appeared to be on a smoother length of track.

Martha sobbed as Percy led her back to the dining car.

“We had better inform the conductor,” said Faith. “Would you mind asking the steward to call him?” She looked at Horace.

“Of course. I’ll explain one of our company is missing and let them know about the open door. I’m sure the conductor can organise a search of the train before we get off. Chloe could still be on board, no matter how unlikely that seems.”

“Yes, there could be a simple explanation for this,” said the major. “Someone might have thought they were opening a window and turned the wrong handle. Or perhaps someone forgot to close the door. If Chloe passed by, she might have fallen out by accident.”

“You think that, Major, if it helps,” Edna said, not unkindly. “Whatever happened, we’re not going to find out standing here, and I’ve got no intention of walking up and down these corridors all night. We’ll be in Bucharest in a few hours, so I’m going to try and get some kip. You coming, Marge?”

"I suppose there's nothing else we can do now. We'll find out what happened soon enough, I'm sure. Goodnight, Major. Would you tell Horace where we've gone?"

"I will. I'll sit with my daughter for a while. She's had quite a shock after being accosted like that by Martha. It won't have helped her mood."

"Probably not," said Marjorie, who had more important things on her mind than Denise's mood.

As they headed back to their sleeping compartment, Edna put into words what was on Marjorie's mind. "Fred scarpered off pretty quickly after Horace got the door closed, did you notice?"

Marjorie wouldn't waste her breath correcting Edna about the man's name. Instead, she replied, "I did. The poor man's had more shocks on this holiday than in many a year, I don't doubt."

"Have it your way, Marge."

"If something has happened to Chloe – which, of course, we don't know yet – Frederick would have no reason to want her dead. At a stretch, I can believe he poisoned Dolores, but not her daughter too."

"Unless they both topped themselves."

"No. Chloe was too happy these past few days, free of the burden of a domineering and demanding mother. She was no more suicidal than you or I."

"If I have to spend much more time with that lot, it might well tempt me to do myself in," retorted Edna.

"Don't joke about such things. It isn't right to tempt fate. Our business now is to find out who had the most to gain from the two women's deaths. At least that will give us motive."

"Unless the second death – if Chloe is dead – was an expedient way of throwing us off the scent, which puts your Fred right back in the frame."

"Why do you dislike him so much?" Marjorie snapped.

"I wouldn't say I don't like him, but he's sneaky. Here one minute, gone the next; always around when there's trouble. By his own admission, he was in the first-class dining car, obviously before the staff changeover as well."

Marjorie had to admit, Edna was right. Frederick had a habit of being in the wrong place at the wrong time, or at least, being unable to give a convincing account of his whereabouts. And there was still the issue of his being seen entering Dolores Hagman's room, and then denying it. Why would he do that if he had nothing to hide?

They arrived at their sleeper and Marjorie lay down immediately. Edna locked the door.

"You can't be too careful with that bunch around," she said, taking her place on her own bed. "See you in a couple of hours."

"Indeed," said Marjorie, falling straight away into a restless sleep.

Chapter 21

Inspector Radu and Danielle Hatmanu were waiting on the platform when the travelling party arrived in Bucharest. The inspector frowned, looking serious, and even Danielle struggled to find a smile when they approached.

Radu barked an order which Horace interpreted. “The police would like us to board the minibus waiting outside without delay.”

“Can’t a man stretch his legs first?” Major Jeffries complained, rubbing his hip then raising the palms of his hands in surrender, following a glower from Inspector Radu.

"Whatever you say, Inspector. Come on, Denise, I don't want any of our belongings going missing, anyway."

The major and a sullen but quiet Denise followed the porter, who had already loaded their luggage onto a trolley. Martha, however, was going nowhere.

"What's the news about Chloe?" She met the inspector's glare with one of her own.

Danielle answered. "We have not found her aboard the train. We have people searching the countryside lining the railway the train would have travelled along within the timescale we were given, but there's a lot of ground to cover. It might be some time before we have news, unless a member of the public reports something. Please do as the inspector says for now. We will meet you at the hotel as soon as we can."

"The police officer's right, Martha," said Percy, taking his wife's arm. "Come on. I could do with breakfast."

"I don't know how you can think of your stomach at a time like this, Percival." Martha shrugged his hand away and marched towards the exit. Everyone headed for the transport, apart from Horace, Marjorie, and Edna. The inspector spoke to Horace in Romanian.

"He's asking if we can tell him anything about Chloe Hagman's disappearance and whether we think it's suicide. It seems they got the message she threw herself off the train."

"Chinese whispers," said Marjorie with a sigh. Danielle raised an eyebrow.

"It's an expression we English use based on a game where a story is altered little by little as it's passed on," explained Horace. "What Marjorie means is that there's no way of anyone knowing what happened to Chloe Hagman at this point."

"She may have jumped or someone may have pushed her off the train. My view is the latter," added Marjorie.

The inspector rubbed his chin following Danielle's translation and asked another question, this time aimed at Marjorie.

"Inspector Radu would like to know if you saw anything leading you to this conclusion."

"Not much, I'm afraid. I saw her go to the toilet at around midnight. I couldn't sleep, so I went to the dining car for a brandy. As it happens, I went to the wrong car as the first-class one was in the opposite direction. I suspect that after using the toilet following an argument with Denise Jeffries, Chloe went to the other car, but we couldn't confirm that because of a shift change. If she was followed and pushed, it could have been by any one of the group already under suspicion."

Horace chatted to the inspector in Romanian, translating what she had said. "I've also told him hardly anyone slept and we were all wandering about the train at some point or other."

"Did you tell him we were the only three to stay in the wrong dining car, leaving them all under suspicion, apart from Major Jeffries? I believe the commotion when Martha was looking for Chloe woke him. Martha gave the impression she didn't know about the first-class dining car, but didn't the steward tell you, Horace, he thought he saw her in there? He definitely saw Percy in there."

Danielle explained what Marjorie had added. Inspector Radu fixed his light-brown eyes on Marjorie and asked another question, which Horace interpreted.

"He asks who you suspect."

Marjorie caught the twinkle in the inspector's eyes and laughed. "It's hard to say. Percy and Denise are the most likely, but who knows?"

"What about Fred?" said Edna.

"Frederick is also a possibility. Although, he didn't try to hide the fact he'd been in the dining car, so it's less likely."

"I can't believe it would be Martha, either," said Edna. "Not with all the fuss she was making. So, I agree, that leaves the firebrand

Denise Jeffries, Percy Gainsborough and your Fred."

"Edna!" Marjorie shot her a glare, much to the amusement of the inspector. It seemed Danielle had been interpreting the conversation.

"I think we had better leave before the others suspect we're up to something," said Horace. "I'll tell them the inspector wanted the story in Romanian. That should keep them quiet for a while."

Inspector Radu nodded and remained on the concourse to speak to the conductor and dining car manager, who were waiting to be interviewed. As soon as they boarded the bus, Denise let her feelings be known.

"Why is it we always have to be kept waiting by you lot? You really think you're something special, don't you? Well, let me tell you—"

"We were merely waiting for the inspector to finish with Horace, that's all. He wanted to hear an account of what had happened during the journey. And," Marjorie said pointedly, "where everyone was from the time Chloe was last seen until Martha discovered her missing. It appears someone told the police she had thrown herself from the train."

"So? That is what happened, isn't it?" Denise wasn't backing down.

"Please take your seats," said Faith. "The driver's been instructed to get us to the hotel as soon as possible. I think it's best not to use conjecture at this point. Let the police do their job."

Marjorie could hear Denise murmuring and complaining to her father as they sat down and for the first part of the journey. The major was only half listening, from what Marjorie could see. His face was ashen. Was he in pain, or did he suspect his daughter might have had something to do with the disappearance of Chloe Hagman?

"What's up, Marge?"

"Nothing's *up*. Why do you ask?"

“You were miles away. Horace asked if you were comfortable.”

“Oh? I apologise, I was just thinking about something.”

“I hope this hotel serves a substantial breakfast. I’m starving,” said Edna.

“It’s always reassuring to know that you have your priorities right, Mrs Parkinton,” said Marjorie with a quiet chuckle.

Chapter 22

An overly upright woman with long brown-streaked white hair stood next to a large suitcase, impatiently tapping a foot on the lobby floor close to the entrance. Despite many offers of help from bellboys, the woman stood her ground. At least, Marjorie noticed, until the rest of their complaining group entered the hotel.

“There they are.” She pointed a long white-gloved finger towards the Hagman party. “Tell them I’m here.” She handed a bellboy a yellow card.

"Come on, Marge. I want to check in before that lot." Edna tried to nudge her along.

"Shush. Wait. I've got a feeling I know who that woman is."

"What woman?" Edna spun around, following her eye line. "Not quite dressed for the sun, is she?" The woman was wearing a long white winter coat, sky-blue slacks, a white hat and round sunglasses.

Marjorie watched with interest the reaction on the face of Martha Gainsborough when the bellboy handed her the card and inclined his head towards the woman. Surprise turned to horror, which turned to pretend-warmth. Percy's response, on the other hand, was downright hostile. His face went a dark shade of purple and his nostrils flared while he and his wife had a heated conversation.

After a few minutes, Martha walked cautiously towards the woman. "Philippa! What a surprise. We weren't expecting to see you."

Philippa Trombone, Marjorie assumed, held out a cool hand. Marjorie had moved in closer, dragging Edna with her to listen in, noticing the woman's thin lips and pale complexion.

"Why would you be expecting me? Dolores is dead. I should be locked away in Oxfordshire, mourning, shouldn't I?" The woman's tone was not dissimilar to that of the late Dolores Hagman. Although controlled, it was no less vindictive.

"It's all been such a distressing time over the past few days. We're all still reeling, and now—"

"What the hell are you doing here, anyway? Can't you see my wife's got enough to worry about without you coming poking your nose in where it's not wanted?"

Philippa prodded the man in his pumped-up chest. "You underestimated me, Percival." She looked around at the major and Denise, who were standing behind the Gainsboroughs. "You all do. I'm here to see they do justice and I won't rest until one of you is rotting inside a Romanian prison."

"Now, now, Philippa. There's no need for this. I know you're upset, but there's no reason to go throwing accusations like that around." Major Jeffries appeared tired and his voice sounded weak. It certainly would not prevent Philippa from causing an even bigger scene than she was already.

Marjorie sidestepped in front of Martha and Percy. Philippa had to lower her head, but even so, Marjorie looked up into the thinnest nostrils she had ever encountered.

How does one breathe through those?

She held out her hand. "How do you do? Are you Philippa Trombone, the lady I spoke to on the telephone?"

Philippa's guard dropped, giving the others time to scoot off towards reception. She held out a hand and took Marjorie's lightly.

"You must be Lady Snellthorpe." Though not friendly, her tone was calmer than it had been a few moments ago.

"Indeed. Let me introduce you to my travelling companions. This is Edna Parkinton, my cousin-in-law."

Philippa gave Edna a curt nod and was going to do an about-turn and follow Martha and crew when Marjorie stopped her.

"And this is Horace Tyler who's been interpreting for the police. He speaks excellent Romanian. Thanks to him, we've been able to keep abreast of the investigation."

A dilemma played its way across Philippa Trombone's face as she weighed up whether to go after the Hagman party or to get an update from Marjorie and company.

"I'd be interested to know what you've found out so far. I've been beside myself with worry."

"It must have taken a great deal of courage to overcome your *agoraphobia* and fly over here," said Edna pointedly. The two women appraised each other, like foxes before a fight, neither wanting to strike the first blow. Marjorie fleetingly wondered how Edna knew about Philippa's claim she suffered from agoraphobia, then remembered she had added that detail when she filled her cousin-in-law and Horace in on her two telephone conversations with the woman.

Oblivious, Horace held out his hand. “Why don’t we all check in and meet down here in an hour? We can tell you where we’ve got to so far. The police who are investigating your friend’s death have followed us down here. I expect they’ll be along later. I’ll introduce you to the inspector leading the investigation.”

Having dropped Horace’s hand as quickly as she had Marjorie’s, Philippa agreed. “At least the police are taking it seriously if they’re down here with you. I’d be happy to meet them, but I don’t have anything else to add other than what I’ve already told them.”

“Nevertheless,” said Marjorie, “I’m certain the inspector would be pleased to hear it from you. Things are never the same second hand, are they?”

“An hour, then.” Philippa swung around, clicking her fingers at the bellboy who had been hovering close by.

"I can tell you now, I don't like her any more than I do that creepy lot," said Edna when the woman had stalked off.

"She's certainly not unlike them, is she? And, by all accounts, she's going to be difficult to handle."

"Why do people click their fingers like that?" said Horace. "It's totally unnecessary. She's lost her best friend, so I'm willing to give her the benefit of the doubt, but I have a feeling she's going to hinder rather than help our investigation."

"Don't worry, Horace. Our Marge will keep Philly Trombone under control. Nice move, by the way," Edna said, nudging Marjorie.

"Yes, I was rather impressed, too. You were swift of foot, Marjorie. I believe your intervention has saved us all some very red faces, not to mention our reputation as we're going to be staying here for a few days."

"It was quite an entrance, wasn't it?" Marjorie chuckled. "I expect it will give the staff something to talk about until the next scandal."

“Indeed. I’m sure they’ve seen far worse,” said Horace. “Do you think she knows about Chloe?”

“How could she?” answered Edna.

“Unless someone told her, but why would they?” said Marjorie.

“They wouldn’t. I think Martha’s learned her lesson, don’t you, Marge?”

Marjorie shook her head. “I think Martha was about to tell her about Chloe when Percy interrupted.”

“He’s met his match with Philly. Did you see how she put him in his place? I thought he was going to have an apoplectic fit.” Edna snorted and Horace guffawed.

Marjorie, meanwhile, headed towards the reception desk, deep in thought.

Chapter 23

It was difficult to unpack when she was feeling this tired, so Marjorie ignored the suitcase that had been conveniently placed on top of the bed. Her eyes brightened at spying familiar teabags along with some fruit tea selections.

Half an hour later, feeling much more alert and ready to face whatever the rest of the day had in store, Marjorie headed downstairs to the lobby. Philippa Trombone occupied the centre of the lobby again, foot tapping, just as she had done earlier. The upright woman had changed into a pair of navy blue slacks and removed the winter coat, but still wore an unseasonal high-necked cream cashmere jumper, making her look even more elongated than she already was.

Marjorie guessed Philippa was around six feet tall. Although a pallor suggested she spent more time indoors than was beneficial for her, she looked otherwise in good health. Marjorie believed one's hair indicated how healthy a person was, and Philippa's, though not a length or colour that suited her at all, had a flourishing sheen to it.

"Hello again," Marjorie deliberately approached from behind, wanting to gauge the other woman's reaction.

It was sharp. "I was beginning to think no-one was coming."

Ignoring the rebuke, Marjorie checked the busy lobby for signs of Horace or Edna. "I take it the others haven't come down yet?"

"I can't imagine what's taking them so long. I managed to shower and change and still arrive on time," Philippa snapped.

Marjorie was not paying much attention to her complaints. Instead, she was trying to estimate how old Philippa was. Dolores had been late sixties, sixty-seven Edna had said, and Marjorie had assumed her friend would be of a similar age, yet Philippa looked older, but moved like someone much younger.

"I'm afraid at our age, when one has been travelling all night, it rather slows one down. You'll have to forgive us for not being quite as vigorous as yourself."

"Horace looks pretty fit to me, although your cousin is a bit on the flabby side."

Marjorie would normally have corrected the cousin mistake, but taken aback by the stranger's rudeness, she found herself instead leaping to Edna's defence. "Edna's been unwell over the past few years, but she's quite robust, I can assure you." Grateful to see her cousin-in-law emerging from the lift with Horace, she said, "Here they are now."

“Apologies for being late. I received a call from Inspector Radu while we were waiting for the lift. It appears the body’s been found.”

“What body?” Philippa squeaked.

“I was going to tell you once we sat down,” said Marjorie. “Chloe Hagman disappeared during the night.”

Philippa rubbed her forehead hard with her gloved hand.

“Look, shall we grab a coffee and we can fill you in on the latest developments? The inspector says it’s a fast-moving investigation, but he’s certain he can draw it to a conclusion very soon.” Horace took Marjorie’s arm and slid her off to the side while Edna led a confused Philippa Trombone towards a table.

“Is it definitely Chloe?”

“Radu seems to think so. I wanted to ask before we start, how much should I tell her?” He inclined his head forwards towards Edna’s reluctant captive.

"As little as possible without making it obvious. I have a feeling we need to keep this woman at arm's length, or she might take us for fools."

"I'll ask you to elaborate on that later."

Horace and Marjorie joined the other two at the table. Noticing Philippa removing her glove, Marjorie saw her thumb about to make contact with her middle finger. Marjorie cut off the clicking by smiling at a nearby waiter who came to their table. Philippa returned the glove to the disappointed hand. If there was such a thing.

They ordered hot drinks, making polite conversation until tea and coffee were served. Then Marjorie eyed Philippa.

"I expect you'll be wanting to know where the police are up to with their investigation. The truth is, we don't really know. What we have discovered so far is that your friend died from cyanide poisoning..." Marjorie paused, but Philippa didn't seem surprised by the news. Martha must have called her again to inform her of the post-mortem results. "As someone administered the cyanide via a hot drink in

Dolores's own flask, anyone could have tampered with it prior to the opera."

"Or during the opera," added Edna.

"Major Jeffries believes Dolores committed suicide," said Horace.

A slight twitch of the left cheek was the only visible reaction Marjorie noticed from Philippa.

"That's ridiculous! Dolores didn't kill herself. She was in fear for her life. That's what she told me. The line was terrible, but I think she may have mentioned someone she used to be close to had got it in for her."

"You didn't mention that when we spoke on the telephone," said Marjorie, fearful that she might have been wrong about Frederick all along.

"It was the shock. I didn't remember what she'd said until I went over the conversation again in my head. I tried calling the police back, but they wouldn't put me through to the person in charge." A tear formed in her left eye before she pursed her thin lips. "That's why I summoned all my strength and came over. The only thing I could get out of the police was that you were being allowed to leave for Bucharest. The person I spoke to had very little command of the English language."

"As opposed to your fluent Romanian," Edna muttered, just loud enough to summon a smirk from Horace.

"I'm amazed they told you the name of our hotel," said Marjorie.

"They didn't. Dolores left me a copy of her itinerary. It's as if she had some sort of premonition."

Marjorie kicked her cousin-in-law's foot under the table before a low snort became a full-blown Edna laugh.

"We're so sorry for your loss." Marjorie wanted to move the conversation away from the imagined to the real. "If you hadn't received the call from Dolores on the night she died, would you have said she was the kind of person who might take her own life?"

Philippa steepled her gloved fingers beneath her chin. “There’s no doubting she’d had a tough couple of years since that rat of an ex went off with some bimbo. Dolores has always been volatile. Until a few months ago, I’d have said she was depressed.”

“Why up until a few months ago?” Edna asked.

“Things started to look up when she got a publishing and film deal for a saga she’d written.”

“And is that where the money you mentioned on the telephone came from?” Marjorie checked.

“Yes. And there was a lot. I told her to go easy, warning her that if the family knew about it, you never knew what they might do. I’ve been fighting a losing battle, and now it looks as though I’ve lost it altogether.”

“Do you think she told her family and friends about this deal?” Marjorie was faithfully clinging on to any hope of Frederick’s innocence.

"No. She wouldn't have risked it. She didn't trust Martha or her scoundrel husband."

"What about Chloe?" Horace quizzed. "Surely she would have told her daughter."

"At one time, she would have. They used to be close, but lately Martha's had Chloe eating out of her hand, if you know what I mean. Chloe... what is this about Chloe being missing and a body being found?"

"Sad business," said Horace. "It seems she may have thrown herself off the train. At least, that's what it looks like. A dog walker stumbled across the body of a woman early this morning, the inspector says. They're waiting for details, but it seems unlikely it would be anyone else."

"Poor Chloe," said Philippa. "What a desperate thing to do. You said the police think they know who killed Dolores?"

All eyes were fixed on Horace. "I can't tell you any more than that. Inspector Radu will be here once he's got more information about the body."

"You said Dolores thought someone she had been close to might kill her, and she was once close to her daughter. That must be it," said Edna, triumphantly. "Chloe killed her mother – and to be honest, if she'd been my mother, I'd have been sorely tempted to do the same – then couldn't live with what she'd done, so she jumped off the train."

"I'd never have imagined it might be Chloe," said Philippa, removing her gloves and placing them on her lap. "But what you say makes sense."

"Why would Chloe kill her mother?" Marjorie asked.

"Doh! You met the woman," Edna said before addressing Philippa. "Sorry, I know she was your friend and all that, but she was a real pain in the butt."

Philippa's eyes narrowed as she switched them from Edna to Marjorie.

"I thought you said on the phone you liked Dolores."

Marjorie kicked Edna again. “I felt we hit it off, yes. Edna doesn’t always take to people straight away, but she doesn’t mean anything by it, and Dolores was rather harsh with her daughter. Someone upset Dolores on the day we arrived – I think you said on the telephone she had argued with Martha – so I don’t imagine we immediately saw the best side of her.”

“Dolores could be a tyrant where Chloe was concerned, but if I’m honest, I suspected the murderer was one of the evil triplets.”

“Meaning Martha, Percy or Denise, I presume?” asked Marjorie.

“Yep, you’ve sussed them already, then? Percy Gainsborough is a two-bit actor who behaves as if he were world famous. He didn’t even scrape by. Martha’s work kept them afloat for years, according to Dolores. Martha fancied herself a writer, submitted manuscript after manuscript to publishers, but was constantly turned down. She directs rubbish plays for the local theatrical society and just about earns enough to live on. And as for Denise Juvenile

Jeffries, she's just a spoiled brat who's never had to grow up. Her temper's hot enough to launch a rocket with an ego to match. She hated Dolores for her success."

"Not to mention your friend's affair with her father while her mother lay dying," challenged Marjorie.

"You've really managed to dig up the dirt, haven't you? It was a fling. It meant nothing to Dolores."

"But it would have made quite an impact on a grieving child, I imagine, so if she hated your best mate, in my book, she had good reason to," said Edna, glaring at Philippa.

"You may not have liked my friend, but at least your cousin saw the good side of her. We all have our faults. I suspect even you, Miss Hoity-Toity."

Before the battle of the wrinklies went any further, Marjorie felt it was time to remove some of the heat. "If Chloe killed her mother, why do you think she would do it now? Cyanide poisoning isn't a spur-of-the-moment type of murder, so she can't have lost her temper and killed her mother in a fit of rage. The death would have been planned down to the tiniest detail."

"The two of them had been at loggerheads for a year, and it had got worse over the past few months since Dolores was no longer financially dependent. Chloe didn't like that, so she could have been planning it prior to the holiday. It would explain why she begged her mother to join them on this trip."

Marjorie felt a bolt of lightning had struck her. "Why would Dolores depend financially on her daughter?"

Philippa sighed heavily. "I might as well tell you, you're bound to find out. Dolores was extravagant. I told you that. When she had money, she spent it like it came out of thin air. Of course, when she was the famous opera singer everyone wanted to see, it didn't matter, but age caught up with her and both the bookings and the money dried up.

"Her ex was wealthy, so it wasn't a problem while they were married, but somehow, he bought her off when they divorced. Dolores wanted immediate money – that's the way she was – so she took a lump sum, and he got the lawyers to tie it up tight so there could be no legal challenges."

"And she frittered the money away," finished Edna. "I almost feel sorry for her."

Philippa nodded. "It was soon gone."

Marjorie asked, "But where did Chloe's money come from?" It also begged the question as to whether Martha's interest in her niece had been as altruistic as it appeared.

"She inherited it from her aunt on her father's side. There were no other living relatives and Connie didn't get on with her brother, who didn't need money anyway, so she left a substantial amount for Chloe and the rest to charity. Some of you," she glared at Edna, "might have been taken in by Chloe. But she wasn't the victim in all of this; Dolores was. I expect what you witnessed was simmering anger over Dolores having to depend on her daughter who – trust me on this – never let her forget it. That was why Chloe resented the fact her mother was financially independent again."

"I see," said Marjorie. "You've given us plenty to think about."

"Yeah, and now it's time for breakfast. I'm starving," said Edna.

Chapter 24

Much to Edna's relief, Philippa didn't join them for breakfast. Percy and Major Jeffries were leaving as they entered the restaurant. At Marge's direction, they joined Fred, who was sitting alone.

Probably moping, thought Edna.

"Have you ordered?" Horace asked Fred as they sat down.

"Just a pot of coffee so far. I don't much feel like eating."

"Well, I do, I'm—"

"Hungry," Marge interrupted her, clearly not willing to hear Edna say 'starving' again. Edna knew full well that some of her expressions irritated her cousin, but Marge would just have to lump them. She wouldn't allow anyone to change her, and she felt certain that in Marge's kinder moments, she would realise she liked her as she was. Edna was unique and intended to stay that way.

"Yeah," was all she said.

On cue, a waitress appeared and took their orders, all of them opting for continental breakfasts. Even Edna couldn't face anything too heavy. Spending fifteen minutes with Philippa Trombone was enough to put anyone off their food.

"I saw you talking to Miss Trombone. Did she have anything interesting to say?" Fred asked.

"Might as well tell you," said Horace, "now it seems the police think they've solved the mystery. Philippa confirms that Dolores rang her on the night she died and we have no reason to doubt it. Apparently, she said the woman was frightened someone she had once been close to was going to kill her."

Fred's head flushed a light shade of red. "You mean me?"

"We thought that at first, but it turns out Dolores and Chloe had once been close, but more recently, they weren't. So, our assumption, and that of the police, is that the daughter killed her mother."

"Then, finding she couldn't live with herself, she jumped off the train," Edna finished.

Fred rubbed his chin, pushing his plate away as he did so. "Is that what the police definitely think, or is it just you?"

"The inspector suggested the theory when he called me earlier..." Horace turned to Marge and Edna. "Sorry I didn't get the chance to say so before, and I didn't want to give too much away until we had sussed Miss Trombone out."

"So Dolores didn't kill herself." Fred sounded relieved.

"It doesn't look like it, but we're still waiting for Inspector Radu to tell us what his official verdict is. I guess we'll know soon enough," said Horace.

"You don't look thrilled, Marge," Edna screwed her eyes up, trying to read her cousin's mind. "What's up?"

"I'm not sure, really. Something doesn't add up. The suitcases and the letter are still puzzling me. Philippa made no reference to Dolores making a run for it. It's as if she didn't know."

"What do you mean?" asked Fred.

"Marge is convinced Dolores Hagman was going to disappear to America because she packed a few too many cases and because of a letter from a publisher in her safe."

"In her safe? How would you know that?"

"Never mind how we know. We just do, and don't look so high and mighty, Mr Self-Righteous, when you lied about being in the diva's room before the opera."

Edna's challenge did the trick. This time, the face and head went a deep shade of crimson. Fred cleared his throat, looking down at his interlocked fingers before addressing Marge.

"I'm sorry."

"It's not me you lied to; it's the police and Horace here."

Fred sighed. "I panicked. It was already looking like the police had it in for me, what with Dolores's friends and family pointing the finger in my direction. I was afraid if I admitted seeing her that afternoon, they would dig deeper and find out more about me."

"Whoa! Hold up," said Edna, incredulously. "What do you mean, more about you?"

"I suppose, if I'm no longer under suspicion—"

"I wouldn't go that far, old chap," said Horace. "We don't know yet."

"In that case, I'd rather not say." Fred's chin jutted out, making him look like a petulant child.

Marge chuckled. The twinkle in her eye caused Edna to raise an eyebrow. Marge turned her attention back towards Fred.

"I take it Dolores didn't give you the answers you were looking for?"

He shook his head. "She did a lot of yelling after I asked the question, along the lines of how dare you turn up after all these years, demanding answers? She even accused me of stalking her. Five minutes in the room with her made me appreciate what a happy life I'd had and how grateful I should be that Dolores did what she did. The woman was paranoid. In the end, I was glad to get out of there; a bit sad at how she'd turned out, but pleased I hadn't married her. When I saw how she treated her daughter, it made me angry."

"If you're going to convince us you had nothing to do with her death," said Marge, "you're going to have to trust us with what else it is you're hiding from the police."

"She's right," said Horace. "Honesty is the best course."

Fred hesitated, refilled his coffee cup, and then clearly made a decision. With eyes fixed on Marge, he declared, “I’m a retired pharmacist.”

“I can see why you would want to hide that fact in view of how the diva died,” Edna chortled. “Let’s hope you’re no longer on the suspect list, or you could very well end up in the slammer.”

“Edna, you’re not helping,” Marge admonished.

“You can see how it looks, though, can’t you?” Edna argued.

“Perhaps it won’t need to come out,” said Horace. “Although you mustn’t lie again if the police ask you about your visit to Dolores, or about what you did for a living.”

“And you must give us your word you had nothing to do with either Dolores or Chloe’s death,” said Marge. Edna noticed how she held Fred’s gaze.

“Yeah. Your word,” said Edna. “Cos we know how trustworthy that is.” She hoped Fred wasn’t taking her and, more importantly, Marge for fools.

"I'm surprised you need to ask, but I suppose we don't really know each other. And as for my word," he glared at Edna, "I'm not in the habit of lying. I told you, I panicked. What would you have done if the tables were turned?"

Edna opened her mouth to answer, but Marge nudged her before pressing Fred again.

"Do we have your word?"

"I assure you, I had nothing to do with either woman's death. I don't carry cyanide around with me on the off chance I might run in to an ex-lover, and I did not know Dolores would be on this trip, or I would never have come. And finally, she was very much alive when I left her room, as you well know, because we were all at the opera."

Nudging Edna again to keep her quiet, Marge continued to address Fred. "Did you see the flask in question when you entered her room?"

"All I saw was a pile of suitcases, like you mentioned. I thought nothing of it at the time, but she was carrying a lot of baggage for a two-week holiday."

"In more ways than one," said Horace sardonically.

"*If* we believe him," Edna emphasised the word *if*, "then it was the mother killed daughter thing."

"Daughter killed mother thing," said Marge.

"Yeah, that. Still, whatever way you look at it, the investigation's over and we can get on with enjoying our holiday. The first thing I need, though, is a bit of sleep. I hardly slept a wink last night."

Marge burst into a fit of giggles.

"What? What did I say now?" Edna asked.

"It's just that..." Marge was apparently fighting a losing battle against the giggles, "it's just... when you snore, you sound like a..." she giggled again.

"Like a what?" Edna demanded.

"A trombone."

"Why's that so funny? Oh, I get it. You're linking my snoring with Philippa Trombone. Hilarious.

Ha, ha," but when Horace laughed, Edna saw the funny side and joined in.

"Sorry to interrupt." Faith appeared at their table. "Inspector Radu's here. He'd like to speak to us all again."

A flicker of concern crossed Fred's brow, which no-one but Edna noticed as Horace and Marge were already gathering themselves together to follow Faith. Edna watched Fred while taking up the rear as they all walked along an endless corridor into a meeting room.

Denise glared as they entered. "Here they are again, keeping everyone waiting as usual."

"As we had no idea we were meeting until Faith fetched us just now, I don't see how you could expect us to be here any earlier," Edna retorted. "My clairvoyance doesn't stretch that far, Miss Mouthy, and to be honest, I'm getting sick and tired of your big gob."

Edna allowed Marge to take her arm. They sat down. The inspector's grin broadened as Danielle interpreted what Edna had just said.

They were seated around a rectangular conference table, alas it was without the usual bottles of water. The police had clearly commandeered the room at short notice.

“Can we get on with this now?” Percy snapped, but the inspector was happy to draw it out for a little longer while he continued a conversation in Romanian with Danielle. Edna noticed Philippa Trombone sitting at the other end of the table with a face like thunder. She was glaring at Martha, whose eyes were red and swollen. Percy looked uncomfortable, clearly not knowing what to say.

Why does Philippa hate that Martha so? Surely she has done no-one any harm.

Finally, the inspector cleared his throat to stop the murmured conversations, which were becoming louder by the minute. He nodded to Danielle.

“I’m sorry to inform you we have discovered the body of Chloe Hagman on a railway embankment. We have confirmed her identity through photographs shown to Mrs Gainsborough, her aunt."

"Her mother." Martha's voice was barely audible.

"Pardon?" asked Danielle.

"I'm Chloe's birth mother. My sister adopted her when I suffered severe postnatal depression following childbirth. They forcibly admitted me to a mental institution. Our parents insisted I wasn't a fit mother, so they took her from me."

A few gasps broke through the silence. Apart from Percy, the only other person who didn't appear surprised was Philippa.

"Why couldn't you just leave it as it was?" she snapped. "No-one needed to know. In every respect, Chloe belonged to Dolores."

"Who controlled her every move and caused her to blindly depend on her, all the time, separating her from me, her proper mother." Martha's voice was rising.

“They were mutually dependent. They couldn’t live with each other, and they couldn’t live without each other.”

“It makes sense now why you doted on her so much,” said Denise to Martha. “It also begs the question: did you kill your sister? You must have hated her.”

Horace and Danielle were telling the inspector of this latest development. Radu was frowning like a man who had just had a case he thought closed burst wide open again.

“Of course Martha didn’t kill Dolores. Don’t be so stupid,” Percy slammed his fist on the table for silence before looking at the inspector and Danielle. “My wife has suffered enough trauma. Can we get on?”

Danielle had a brief conversation with her boss before addressing the group. “We discovered something else about the night of the opera. It appears that a woman matching Miss Chloe Hagman’s description asked an usher to fill a flask with hot water. The usher saw her adding a powder to the water. He remembers how an older woman – we believe this was Mrs Dolores Hagman – snatched the flask from the younger woman's hand, and then he watched them head towards the exit."

Martha's bloodshot eyes widened and Percy's were on stalks.

"What are you suggesting?"

"It appears Chloe Hagman mixed the fatal solution drunk by her mother. We believed – still believe, despite what we have just heard about Miss Hagman's birth – that Miss Hagman killed her mother before committing suicide."

"No. I don't accept it. I won't accept it," said Martha. "Chloe adored Dolores." Martha looked at Fred. "I'd been ill for some time and struggling to cope with the baby. They admitted me to hospital on the day of your wedding. My parents called Dolores and pleaded with her to take the baby. Dad was ill with Parkinson's. I didn't know about any of this until much later. Don't you see? Whatever anyone else thinks, I was grateful to Dolores. We were sisters."

"Grateful to her?" Philippa's voice was incredulous. "You hated her. She told me you resented her for bringing up Chloe and siding with your parents over the issue. You made her life hell, phoning at all hours, then hanging up. You thought she didn't know it was you, her mad sister. She knew, all right."

"Enough!" Percy yelled. "Don't speak to my wife like that. Come on, darling, I think we're finished here."

"Are we free to go, Inspector?" asked the major.

Danielle told them they were. Inspector Radu shook Horace's hand, also shaking Marge and Edna's before leaving.

"Thank goodness that's over," said Faith. "We're finally free to join the river cruise the day after tomorrow. I'm sorry about the disruption to our schedule." She almost floated from the room, leaving the quartet she had brought in from the breakfast room behind.

"It's really over, then," said Fred.

"Hardly," said Marge. "Now we must find the actual killer."

Edna stared at her in disbelief.

Chapter 25

Fifteen minutes after Marjorie dropped her bombshell, the four of them were huddled around a small table in a quiet bar.

"You can't just say things like that, Marge, with no explanation," Edna berated her. "Why can't you just accept what the police say happened rather than trying to complicate matters?"

"Because we are dealing with a calculating, ruthless killer who will stop at nothing to get what they want."

"And what is it they want?" asked Horace, taking a sip of Scotch.

"When we find that out, we'll know who it is," Marjorie stated.

"If I didn't know you better, Marge Snellthorpe, I'd say you'd been taking my medication." Edna sniggered. "So you don't know who killed those two women, or why, but you can't believe it was the way the police explained. Even though they have a witness who saw Chloe mix the drink that poisoned her mother."

"Yes. But did she do it deliberately?" Frederick asked, looking at Marjorie. "You don't believe she did." Considering the news he'd just received from Martha, Frederick looked remarkably calm. *I expect he's relieved to finally discover why Dolores abandoned him.*

Addressing his statement, Marjorie said, "No, I don't think Chloe knew what was in the powder. All we know is that she poured a sachet of powder into hot water. Where that powder came from – that's what we should be asking. I'm convinced Chloe was given the powder meant for her mother by someone else. What we don't know is whether she killed herself. If so, was it because she later realised what she'd done and couldn't face the consequences? Or she couldn't handle the truth: that the person who told her to administer the powder was a killer? And if she didn't kill herself, did the same person who gave her the powder also kill Chloe? Those are the two other things we need to investigate.

"The fact of the matter is, we all met the downtrodden daughter. Whatever picture Philippa Trombone tries to paint, that woman was incapable of thinking for herself, let alone planning a murder. I don't believe she's ever held down a job for long or been allowed to live her life, except in the shadow of her domineering mother and, to some extent, her resentful aunt, who we now discover is her birth mother."

"But surely that gives her even more of a motive, Marge? Maybe she just snapped. People do that. They tolerate years of abuse, and then a switch flicks inside of them and they lash out."

"Now that, I could believe," said Horace. "But what Marjorie says makes sense. This wasn't a spur-of-the-moment killing – the sort you so eloquently describe," he flashed a smile at Edna, "but a pre-planned down-to-the-last-detail poisoning. Done in a way that would make it look like a heart attack."

"I agree," said Frederick. "Cyanide's the ideal poison in such a case. An older woman with an unhealthy lifestyle, no-one would blink twice."

"Except, the killer didn't anticipate Dolores becoming frightened and calling her best friend on the night of the murder," said Edna, nodding. "But the brief impression we got of Chloe Hagman doesn't rule her out as the killer. She could have been exactly like Trombone says. We knew nothing about her, and first impressions aren't always the right ones."

Marjorie picked up a teacup and brought the satisfying liquid to her mouth. "I'm so pleased this hotel serves better tea. It's heavenly."

"I agree," Frederick grinned, lifting his cup in a toast. "To English tea."

"I hate to cast a cloud over the tea admiration society, but for one thing, the stuff you're drinking is probably from India or Sri Lanka. And what the heck's tea got to do with Dolores and possibly Chloe Hagman's murders?" Edna huffed, blowing air from her puffed-out cheeks.

"I prefer coffee myself," said Horace, "when I'm not drinking Scotch."

"That's not Scotch, it's a Russian whisky. I saw the bottle." Edna now sounded exasperated.

"Party pooper," said Marjorie. "However, you're quite right. Our current refreshments have nothing to do with the murders, but they do help keep one's brain alert after being up all night. Apart from the whisky, that is."

"Right, Marge, I'm going to humour you for a minute. Who do you think killed Dolores if Chloe didn't, and neither did chief suspect number two here because he's *given his word*?"

Marjorie noticed Frederick's forehead crinkle at Edna's sarcasm. "I can't tell you because I don't know. I think we can rule out the major, which leaves us with three suspects."

"My money's on Percy or Denise," said Horace. "I can't see the gentle Martha killing her sister, and after what we've learnt about Chloe's birth – which Philippa Trombone appeared to know about – she definitely wouldn't have killed her daughter. At least it explains why she doted on the girl."

"Unless," said Frederick thoughtfully, "she killed her sister out of resentment so she could have her daughter back. It must have been tough, especially as she and Percy haven't been able to have children."

"Who told you that?" snapped Edna.

"He did. That day, when we stopped for lunch and Horace insisted on paying the bill, me and Percy got chatting. He's not as bad as he makes out. Have you noticed how he always backs down when his wife tells him to? He loves her dearly, and a man like that is hardly likely to be a murderer."

"On the contrary," said Marjorie. "Love is sometimes a powerful motive for murder, as is jealousy. He may have resented Chloe, but he most certainly hated Dolores, about whom he made his feelings quite clear."

"So you think it's more likely to be Percy than Denise?" Edna asked.

"Well, he is a fan of Shakespeare, many of whose plays are nothing if not violent. Poisons and potions are a favourite of the Bard's, I believe, although I don't remember any of the poisons of choice being cyanide. Nevertheless, Percy would be familiar with the idea of poison as a lethal weapon."

"Good point, Marge. I can't say I've taken to the man. Up his own backside, as we say in the north."

"Mm," said Marjorie, frowning at Horace for snorting with laughter. "Perhaps you could keep that imagery to yourself."

"If it's as you say," said Horace, "why didn't Chloe go to the police?"

"I've been asking myself that question. She may have been too afraid. The woman was rather pathetic. Perhaps she believed they would arrest her without question. Unless she was protecting the real killer, which would point towards Martha or Denise, whom she seemed close to. Heaven knows why in the latter case. I'm not convinced her mood was low even though Faith thought it was."

Edna pouted. "I still think it's what the police say, for the reasons we already know. Chloe was in seventh heaven after her mother died, remember that. Maybe what she did finally hit her last night and she couldn't live with herself. But for now, Marge, I'm going to bed. I need me beauty sleep."

After Edna had walked rather unsteadily to the lift, Horace asked, "Should I tell Inspector Radu what you suspect? Although I'm not sure how receptive he'll be. He's probably on a flight to Cluj by now."

"No, I think we need to hold off on that one until we have more information about what it was Dolores was running away from and whether she really was intending to go to America. I didn't get the impression Philippa knew anything about that. It seems odd Dolores wouldn't tell her best friend."

"I can't see her not knowing," said Horace. "Perhaps that's why Dolores wanted her on this trip: to say goodbye."

"Did she want Philippa to come?" asked Frederick. "I thought the family and friends didn't like the woman."

"Miss Trombone told me on the telephone that Dolores had invited her, but she refused because she suffers from anxiety and doesn't go out much."

"Edna would say to take that with a pinch of salt." Horace laughed. "She says the woman's made a remarkable recovery, flying over here all by herself."

"On the other hand," challenged Frederick, "it shows a substantial amount of courage and a deep love for her late friend."

Marjorie felt she was missing something, but couldn't clear enough fog from her brain to make any sense of her thoughts.

"I'm sorry, gentlemen, but I think I'm going to take a quick nap before lunch. We'll resume this conversation later. I fear we need to get to the bottom of this case before we start the next leg of our journey. Shall we meet in the lobby before lunch?"

"Would one o'clock suit?" suggested Horace.

Marjorie nodded, suddenly feeling a little wobbly as she stood up.

"Let me escort you to your room," said Frederick, taking her arm.

Chapter 26

Edna descended one of the grand marble staircases, arriving downstairs earlier than expected. Sleep had evaded her, despite her eyelids feeling as if they were laden with lead. It was the first opportunity she'd had to peruse the lobby of the Bucharest Grand Hotel, as Philippa Trombone's appearance had dominated everyone's attention when they'd arrived.

The lobby was chic in every sense of the word, with shiny tiled marble floors and comfortable chaise-longue type seating tastefully placed to allow for comfort. The decor was neutral with furniture and blinds adding smatterings of brown. She had flicked through the information in her suite and planned to visit the shopping gallery before their river cruise departure. That's if Marge would allow them to relax, instead of behaving like she was some sort of off-duty detective.

She should know better at her age. The only reason Edna was humouring her now was because Horace had said they should take Marge seriously after she had been right the last time.

Edna strolled out to the summer terrace and ordered ice-tea. Shortly after sitting down, she noticed Martha and Percy at a table not far away from her. They hadn't seen her come in and seemed engaged in an intense discussion, Percy waving a letter in the air every so often. It wasn't difficult to make out what he was saying, with a foghorn for a *bouche*.

"It can't be true. Why would she do this to you? It's lies, damned lies."

Martha must have told him to keep it down because he continued his complaint in a more restrained fashion. Not wanting to miss out on eavesdropping, Edna picked up her tea and surreptitiously sidled past a pillar, taking a seat on the other side with her back to their table.

"I knew she could be deceptive, but I never imagined for one minute she would go back on her word." Martha was speaking. "After her divorce, we agreed that should anything happen to either one of us, we would leave the remains of our estates to each other—"

"You should never have trusted her. That woman was pure evil. If I'd known about this, I never would have—" Percy stopped.

"Never would have what, Percy? Please tell me you had nothing to do with their deaths."

Percy didn't get to reply because someone else turned up, clearly interrupting their conversation.

"Come to crow, have you?" Percy said angrily.

"What drivel are you talking now?" Edna recognised Philippa Trombone's icy tone.

"Martha's had a letter from the family lawyer. What did you do to wheedle your way into what should have belonged to my wife?"

"You mean after the death of your beloved sister-in-law and your niece, or should I say, stepdaughter?" An evil cackle emanated from the Trombone woman, reminding Edna of Cruella De Vil in *101 Dalmatians*. She had to resist the urge to turn and slap her.

"Don't," Martha's cracked voice pleaded.

"Now see what you've done. Have you no respect? My wife has lost her sister and her, erm... daughter in the matter of a few days. Why don't you just leave us alone?"

Edna couldn't resist craning her neck to see what would happen next. Percy was standing, his large frame bearing down on the long, spindly woman with the streaked hair.

"I'm warning you—"

"Warn away, Percival. I'm not afraid of you; you're a pathetic, washed-up two-bit actor who was hoping to cash in on his wife's good fortune. Well, I can tell you now, Dolores saw what was coming from miles away. She had no intention of leaving what she had worked for all these years to a pair of spongers."

"I didn't want her money, I wanted my daughter back," Martha screeched.

Edna looked around, but there were no other guests on the terrace. The waiters were keeping their distance.

"But I'd have been happy to share her. Now they're both gone. If you did this, Percy, I'll never forgive you." Martha scraped her chair back and stormed into the hotel.

Percy, purple-faced, eyes bulging, teeth gritted, said, "I'll get you for this." He then stomped after his wife.

Philippa cackled loudly, calling after him, "Not from prison, you won't."

Edna cleared her throat loudly. "Having fun?" she said.

Philippa peered around the pillar. "I didn't see you skulking behind there. I suppose you heard all that?"

"Every word," said Edna. "I take it you're inheriting Dolores's estate?"

Philippa gave an evil smirk, her eyes narrowing. "What's that to you?"

"Nothing. Nothing at all. I am intrigued by one thing, though. You told my cousin someone was after this new money and you clearly suspect Percy Gainsborough. But, where did the money come from?"

Philippa shrugged. "I told you earlier, it came from a publishing and film deal Dolores signed."

"That's why she was running off to America?"

The mask slipped momentarily before Philippa answered, "The deal was American, but I don't know where you get that impression. Dolores wasn't going anywhere."

Edna stood, fixing her eyes firmly on the now less-assured Philippa Trombone's. "Dolores was going to America to start a new life without you, and without her so-called family and friends. It's a shame Percy appears to have killed her before she got the chance."

Philippa straightened, a malicious smile crossing her face. "He'll get what's coming to him. I hope they lock him up in a Romanian jail for a very long time. I don't think he'll find it quite as cosy as those we have in England, do you?"

"You might have got the money, but you'll die a lonely old woman," Edna said.

"You'd be surprised what money can buy. Now, if you'll excuse me, I have a meeting with the police and a flight to catch."

Philippa Trombone was a person who always had to have the last word, Edna suspected as she watched the upright woman march back towards the lobby. Edna followed after her and arrived in the lobby just as Horace and Fred appeared.

"You'll never guess what I've just overheard. I'd better ring Marge first. She won't want to miss this."

Chapter 27

The telephone woke Marjorie from a deep sleep. She was running late for lunch, but a thought had come to her in between dreams that she had to follow up.

"You go on into lunch," she said to Edna. "I have another telephone call to make. I'll join you as soon as I can."

"Well, hurry up, 'cos you've missed a right fracas." Edna put the telephone down before Marjorie got the opportunity to ask what she meant.

I'll find out soon enough, I suppose.

Marjorie picked up the receiver again and asked the receptionist to put her through to the Platinia in Cluj. She waited patiently until a female voice came on the line, speaking in broken English.

"Hotel Platinia. What help can I give?"

"I wondered if it would be possible to speak with Nelu. I'm so sorry, I don't know his surname."

There was a pause at the other end. "You mean Nelu Florescu? Waiter?"

"Yes, that's him. He was so attentive when I was staying at your lovely hotel. I'm sorry to trouble you, but might I have a word?"

"Moment please, Lady Snellthorpe..." The receptionist in Bucharest had obviously given her name to the person on the other end.

After a few minutes, Nelu came on the line. "Lady Snellthorpe? Is everything okay?"

"Yes, Nelu, but I need to ask you something. Are we being overheard?"

"No, Simona is helping guests checking in." He lowered his voice. "What is it?"

"I need to ask a favour. It's very important. In fact, it's a matter of life and death. You see, Mrs Hagman did not commit suicide; she was murdered."

"But how can I help?"

"Does the hotel still have her belongings?"

"Yes, but there's a police officer on the way to collect them."

"Then we must act quickly, Nelu. In her things, you will find a letter postmarked from the United States. I need you to take a photograph of that letter and send it to this number." Marjorie reached inside her handbag to pull out her address book in order to look up her own mobile phone number.

"But, Lady Snellthorpe, I'm not sure I can." Nelu sounded panicky.

"If you don't, someone will get away with murder. The police think the wrong person is responsible. I don't have time to go into details about that now. Please do as I ask."

Marjorie could feel her heart pounding as the young man on the other end of the phone hesitated.

"Okay. Let me have your number. I'll do what I can."

"Thank you, Nelu. I'll wait to hear from you."

Marjorie freshened up in the bathroom and hunted out her mobile phone from the bottom of her suitcase. She switched it on, but it was dead.

"Blast! Where did I put that charger?" After ten minutes, she sat on the bed, defeated. She had forgotten to pack it. Mobile telephones had never been her priority, but her son Jeremy insisted she always carried one with her in case of emergencies. It had been the first thing she packed to make sure she would remember to bring it, but she hadn't thought to put the charger in the suitcase. She daren't risk calling the Platinia again in case Nelu was in the middle of going through the dead woman's belongings. She would hate for him to get caught. He was taking enough risk already. There was nothing for it but to ask Edna if she or any of the others had a charger that would fit her phone.

Horace, Frederick and Edna were finishing lunch when she arrived.

"There you are, Marge. Here, sit next to me. You'll never guess what you missed. Have you eaten?"

"No, I haven't eaten. As you know, I slept for longer than expected. I'm not very hungry at the moment, but I'd like a coffee."

"Things must be bad if she needs coffee," said Edna, pouring some into the empty teacup at Marjorie's place setting.

"What did I miss that's so exciting?"

"I witnessed a showdown between the Gainsboroughs and the Trombone woman."

Marjorie felt her eyebrows rise. "How interesting."

"And I know who killed Dolores and Chloe."

"So it wasn't murder/suicide, then?" Marjorie couldn't resist, despite herself.

"Give over, Marge. I've just been telling the guys, I was right all along. It was Percy."

Marjorie frowned. "Whatever gives you that idea?"

"He as good as confessed to his wife before Philippa Trombone showed up and more or less accused him."

"I think you had better tell me the whole story," said Marjorie, not quite following where Edna was going with this.

"I overheard Percy and Martha having a not too happy discussion about something in Dolores's will. It turns out Philippa Trombone is inheriting everything... Why don't you look surprised?"

"Please continue," said Marjorie.

"Anyway, just before Trombone arrived, he confessed."

"To killing Dolores and Chloe?" Marjorie quizzed.

"Not quite. He was about to, but as I said, she interrupted him."

"What did he say? Exactly."

"He said if he'd known – presumably about the will – he wouldn't have... and then he stopped. Martha asked if he'd killed them, but he didn't get the chance to answer. Can't you see? Philippa was right – although I hate to admit to that obnoxious woman being right about anything. It's all about the money."

"I agree that it's all about the money, but I don't believe Percy is the killer. Where did they go after this confrontation?"

"I don't know. It wouldn't surprise me if the Gainsboroughs and the Jeffries take the next flight home. Percy will want to evade the police. Philippa said she was going for a meeting with the police before flying home."

"We can't have any of them leaving the country. We haven't got a moment to lose. Do any of you have a charger for this phone?" Marjorie took the mobile from her handbag.

"You've gotta be kidding, Marge. That's an antique."

"It's imperative I get this phone powered up," Marjorie turned to Horace.

"Come on," he said. "Reception will have a charger tucked away somewhere. People leave them behind all the time."

The four of them hurried over to reception where Horace spoke to a manager, who led them into a room off the side and searched through a drawer. He eventually found what he was looking for and plugged the phone in to a charger. Moments later, it pinged to life. Several other pings followed the first.

Marjorie handed it to Horace.

"What am I looking for?" he asked.

"A message with a photograph sent today from a Romanian telephone number."

Horace raised his eyebrows, but worked his way through her messages. "You need to contact your son and let him know you're safe. Ah, here it is." He pressed a few digits. "Your phone's too old to show the attachment and there's no screen enlarger. I'll take the sim out and ask the manager to connect it to a computer."

Marjorie hadn't a clue what he was talking about, but nodded. Ten minutes later, the manager had called an IT whizz – one of the young receptionists – to access the documents attached and print them off.

"There's another message from the same chap called Nelu," said Horace. "He says you were right and to be careful. He's contacting the police."

"We had better see what he means," said Frederick, removing three pages of documents from the printer. The first was the letter from the publishing agent that Marjorie had already seen. But the second and third were more revealing: letters from Dolores Hagman herself.

Chapter 28

“Good God,” said Horace. He scanned through the longer of the two letters before reading it out loud to the others.

“Could you tell us where Miss Trombone is meeting with the police?” Marjorie asked the manager. He led Marjorie and company to a meeting room. Inspector Radu and Danielle were there, along with Philippa Trombone, Faith Weathers and the remains of the Hagman party. There was a lot of shouting going on when they entered.

Denise rolled her eyes. “Here they come again. The Fantastic Four. What are you doing here?”

Ignoring her, Horace spoke earnestly with the inspector in Romanian. The company looked on, fidgeting in their seats. Denise Jeffries continued firing proverbial daggers at the interlopers.

“Over to you, Lady Marjorie,” Horace said, sitting down.

“What’s she got to do with any of this? If I’m being accused of murder, I want to get this cleared up before we listen to any more nonsense.” Percy’s purple face looked as though it was about to explode. His lips were swollen and he stood up, slamming his fist down on the table.

Inspector Radu said nothing, but motioned for him to sit down. Once Percy obliged, the inspector whispered something to Danielle, who moved to stand in front of the door.

Marjorie cleared her throat. “I’ve just received information that will clarify what you are all wondering: who killed Dolores and Chloe Hagman.” Murmurs went around the room, but all eyes remained fixed on Marjorie. “Dolores was using this holiday as a means of escape from a blackmailer who, it turns out, is also a ruthless killer. I noticed something odd about her room: the number of cases she had with her. She was going to fly to America the morning after the opera."

"No way. You've got that idea from your fat cousin," Philippa snapped. Edna didn't give the insult any response, and Marjorie admired her for it. Philippa continued, "Look, Inspector, I've told you who the killer is. If you don't want to listen to me, I have a plane to catch." She got up and made her way to the door, but Danielle didn't budge.

"Sit down, will you?" snapped Denise. "The sooner we hear this, the sooner we get out of here."

Philippa reluctantly returned to her seat. Inspector Radu nodded for Marjorie to continue.

"Unfortunately for Dolores, the killer had guessed what she was up to and spiked her vanilla chocolate with cyanide."

"Chloe." Martha looked down at her hands, tears falling over her cheeks.

"Chloe gave her the drink, but someone else had already added poison to the powder – someone who knew she liked vanilla chocolate as a treat during a night out. If it hadn't been the night of the opera, it would have been some other time."

"Who would do such a thing?" asked the major.

"I'm coming to that," said Marjorie. "This same person then pushed Chloe off the train in order to inherit the fortune Dolores had come into. It was all about the money."

"You see, Inspector, that's what I've been telling you. That man," Philippa pointed at Percy, "killed my best friend, thinking his wife was going to inherit. I caught them discussing it this afternoon. Ask her. She was listening in." Philippa's pointing finger moved to Edna, who shot her an 'as if I'm going to help you' look.

"You overplayed your hand, Miss Trombone," said Marjorie, glaring at the obstinate woman. "What you didn't realise was that Dolores had written a letter." She held up the papers in her hand. "May I?" she checked with the inspector, who nodded.

Marjorie read:

"Dear Martha and Chloe,

"If you're reading this letter, I will already be dead. She will have killed me and will be hoping to keep the money.

"First of all, I need to apologise. You won't find it easy to forgive me, but that's up to you. You, Martha, asked me to submit your manuscript to a contact I have in America. I did as you asked, but I lied when I told you it had been rejected. When I read the piece, I knew it was a winner. I was broke, bitter, and angry, so when I sent it off, I put my name on it. The agent loved it and sealed a lucrative deal with a hefty advance for worldwide books and film rights. They will publish the first part of the saga this year and filming starts next year.

"I changed the name on the manuscript, but you would have recognised it when it came out. By that time, you would have Chloe back in exchange for what I did. She's what you've always wanted, anyway. Fair deal, if you ask me, after all the years I put into bringing her up, and the personal cost.

"As you know, over the past year or so, I've been in contact with an old friend. I didn't realise until it was too late, I was being duped. One night, I had too much to drink (not unusual, I know) and told her what I'd done. She's been blackmailing me ever since. I've had to change my will to give her and Chloe an equal share of my estate, including the royalties. She has a copy of the will. It was the only way to keep her quiet, but I've been trying to escape her clutches.

"When you mentioned the holiday, it offered me a lifeline. A way of getting away without her realising what I was doing. If you're reading this, though, she's cottoned on to my scheme and found a way of ending my life.

"What I'm going to say next, you'll have to take my word for. My plan was to change the will back once I got to America, leaving everything to Chloe and, in the event of her death, to you,

Martha. I’m sorry it didn’t work out. I would have loved to see my name in lights again. You know there’s nothing I’ve wanted in life more than fame and fortune.

“At least this letter will put Philippa Trombone away and the confession should be enough to restore your rights. I’m sorry about the mess I’ve left you with. I know you’ll take care of Chloe.

“Your sister, Dolores.”

The room was silent apart from gentle sobbing coming from Martha. “I'd got Chloe back," she murmured. "We loved each other. Dolores knew how much I wanted to be a writer and stole that from me too...”

“That's what a nasty person she was,” sneered Philippa, showing that she herself was ten times as nasty. Then she seemed to realise what she'd said. “Anyway, it’s a lie. I wasn’t in Cluj. How could I poison the powder? I only arrived in Romania this morning. Besides, I’m the one who alerted the police.”

"Yes, you did," said Marjorie. "Greed was your biggest mistake. If you had settled for the fifty per cent, you would have got away with Dolores Hagman's murder. But it wasn't enough, was it? You wanted it all. You doctored the sachets before Dolores left for the holiday, knowing it would be the long-suffering Chloe who mixed her the drink. And even if Dolores had administered it herself, everyone would have assumed the unhealthy diva had suffered a heart attack.

"When you heard you had got away with your evil plot, and realised Dolores had unwittingly provided you with a masterstroke where you could take all the money. I expect the real reason for her call was to let you know she had arrived safely or some such thing, hoping by doing so, to allay any suspicions of her escape plan. Or perhaps it was part of the blackmail deal that Dolores had to keep in touch, so she made sure to do so until she had well and truly escaped your clutches. I'm assuming you didn't know the name of her literary agent, so once she had vanished, there was no damage you could do as no-one would know where to find her. You knew the call to you would show up on the dead woman's phone so you called the police, pouring suspicion on Dolores's death, no doubt hoping poor Chloe would be arrested immediately. Then, when you heard the police had released us and suspected suicide, you flew to Cluj – not to Bucharest – and caught the night train. I heard your pompous voice admonishing a porter for not being careful enough with your luggage, but it was you who wasn't careful.

"No doubt you contacted Chloe with some ruse, perhaps telling her not to trust anyone and arranging to meet. She wouldn't have suspected you of putting poison in the vanilla chocolate; she most likely believed her mother had committed suicide when the major suggested it. The poor girl was relieved at getting her life back, but you didn't give her the opportunity to enjoy it. You met her on the train and pushed her onto the tracks in the dead of night before sneaking back to your sleeper."

"But how did she get to the hotel before us?" asked Denise.

"She knew we would be delayed at the station while we collected our luggage. I expect when she saw the police, she realised that gave her even more time. She was one person, travelling alone. All she had to do was hail a taxi and arrive at the hotel as if from the airport. There she played the impatient distraught friend. Isn't that right, Miss Trombone?"

"You'll never prove any of this. All you've got is a letter from an embittered dead woman."

"Oh, I think you should give the police more credit. You will have left evidence in your home. There will be sums of money transferred between accounts. CCTV footage of you in Cluj. A flight to Cluj, rather than Bucharest, will be confirmed, and you will have passed through passport control. I expect you bought your train ticket using your credit card, so confident were you that you could dupe everyone and implicate Mr Gainsborough in both deaths if the murder/suicide theory didn't go to plan."

"Yeah," said Edna, no longer able to hold herself back. "And as you said earlier, Cruella, we can only hope you spend a long time in a Romanian prison."

There was a lot of chattering and cheering after the police had handcuffed Philippa and led her from the room. Even Denise shook their hands. Martha, sadly, was left to her grief, but with a loving husband, she would no doubt get her life back.

Marjorie felt exhausted and suddenly hungry.

"I think I'll have a late lunch."

"We'll come with you, Marge."

Whoopee, she thought, but said, "That will be nice."

Chapter 29

It was the first peaceful meal they had been able to enjoy since arriving in Romania. The food was delicious, and with word quickly getting round that they had solved a double homicide, they were treated like royalty.

Frederick had been quiet over dinner. Marjorie knew why. Before they had come in, she had handed him the second of the two letters: a handwritten note, scrawled by Dolores sometime after he had left her room on the day of the opera. It was meant to be an addendum to the first letter in the event of her death, but Marjorie felt only he should see it.

The note said that she had just seen the only man she had ever loved; the man her parents had robbed her of so she could take care of her sister's daughter. There was also an apology to Chloe for treating her contemptuously over the years; it appeared that it was resentment at Dolores giving up her true love for her. The letter finished with an appeal that should something happen to her, Frederick be told the truth and that she was sorry.

"Now that's what I call a good meal," said Edna, patting her stomach. "I have to hand it to you, Marge, you did it again. When did you first suspect it was the Trombone witch?"

"When she arrived at the hotel. As you pointed out in your usual forthright way, she had made a miraculous recovery for one suffering agoraphobia, which is a debilitating condition. Then it was the voice. It came to me when I was napping: the memory of the woman at the station last night who had the same sharp tone. I called Nelu, hoping there would be airline tickets among Dolores's possessions. I never expected a message from the grave. Without it, we would have had more problems proving Trombone guilty."

"I have no doubt you would have come up with a cunning plan," said Horace. "You're a sleuthing genius and I salute you." He raised his glass.

"One thing that bothers me," said Edna. "Why did she plagiarise her sister's work?"

"Dolores lived beyond her means. Any allowance she had from her daughter would never be enough to give her back the life she craved. Only the plagiarised manuscript could do that. Plus, her letter said it; she longed to see her name in lights again."

"A horrid thing to do to one's flesh and blood," said Horace.

"I agree, but she felt Martha and Chloe had robbed her of her life and any chance of happiness," said Frederick. "It doesn't excuse what she did, but it goes some way to explaining it."

Marjorie knew now he was going to be all right. He was a forgiving man who, unlike Dolores, wouldn't let 'what ifs' rob him of the rest of his life.

Faith appeared once they had finished desserts. "I thought I'd let you know the others are going home. They won't be joining us for the river cruise."

"I'll drink to that," said Edna.

Horace snorted loudly.

"There's something else," said Faith.

Marjorie waited, expectantly. "Not more delays, I hope?"

"No. Nothing like that. Major Jeffries had booked another tour with us to the Scottish Highlands. It includes flights to Inverness and tickets for four people to join a coach tour with accommodation stops at various places, including Loch Ness." Faith cleared her throat. "The tour starts in six weeks, and the major doesn't believe Percy and Martha will be up to it. He wants to thank you for solving the murders and has asked me to pass on the holiday to you four, if you'd like it?"

"Wow, Marge! That would be great, wouldn't it? The Fab Four Go Again."

"Sounds like an Enid Blyton title to me," said Horace. His eyes sparkled. "What about it, Marge?"

"Don't you start with the Marge thing, or it will be a definite no."

"What about you, Fred?" Horace nudged their new friend.

"It's Frederick." He sighed. "I suppose someone will have to provide Marjorie with sane company."

"Is that a yes?" asked Faith. "I'll be there too."

"It appears to be a yes," said Marjorie. She would never admit to it, but she was finding herself very much enjoying her present company. Even Edna.

THE END

Author's Note

Thank you for reading *Murder at the Opera House*, the first book in the brand new Lady Marjorie Snellthorpe Mystery series. If you have enjoyed it, please leave an honest review any platform you may use.

If you would like to read the prequel to the series, the novella, *Death of a Blogger* is available for free when you sign up for my newsletter where you will receive news and offers once a month. If you prefer not to subscribe to newsletters, the book is available to purchase via the majority of eBook stores or to borrow, on request, from libraries. Print and audiobook versions are also available

To find out what happens to our feisty pensioners next, you can preorder the next-in-series *Murder in the Highlands.*

Discover where the Lady Marjorie character began; check out the Rachel Prince Mystery series.

Books by Dawn Brookes

Lady Marjorie Snellthorpe Mysteries

Death of a Blogger (Prequel Novella)

Murder at the Opera House

Murder in the Highlands

Rachel Prince Mysteries

A Cruise to Murder

Deadly Cruise

Killer Cruise

Dying to Cruise

A Christmas Cruise Murder

Murderous Cruise Habit

Honeymoon Cruise Murder

A Murder Mystery Cruise

Hazardous Cruise

Captain's Dinner Cruise Murder

Corporate Cruise Murder (Available to preorder)

Carlos Jacobi

Body in the Woods

The Bradgate Park Murders

Body at the Jewry Wall (coming soon)

Memoirs

Hurry up Nurse: Memoirs of nurse training in the 1970s

Hurry up Nurse 2: London calling

Hurry up Nurse 3: More adventures in the life of a student nurse

Keep in touch:

Sign up for my no-spam newsletter at:

https://www.dawnbrookespublishing.com

Follow me on Facebook:

https://www.facebook.com/dawnbrookespublishing/

Follow me on Twitter:

@dawnbrookes1

Follow me on Pinterest:

https://www.pinterest.co.uk/dawnbrookespublishing

Acknowledgments

Thank you to my editor Alison Jack, as always, for her kind comments about the book and for suggestions, corrections and amendments that make it a more polished read.

Thanks to my immediate circle of friends who are so patient with me when I'm absorbed in my fictional world and for your continued support in all my endeavours.

Thank you so much to my Advance Reader Team for comments and support.

About the Author

Award winning author, Dawn Brookes is author of the *Rachel Prince Mystery* series, combining a unique blend of murder, cruising and medicine with a touch of romance. She is also author of the Carlos Jacobi crime series and the Lady Marjorie Snellthorpe Mystery series.

Dawn holds an MA in Creative Writing with Distinction and has a 39-year nursing pedigree. She loves to travel and takes regular cruise holidays, which she says are for research purposes! She brings these passions and a love of clean crime to her writing.

The surname of her Rachel Prince protagonist is in honour of her childhood dog, Prince, who used to put his head on her knee while she lost herself in books.

Bestselling author of *Hurry up Nurse: memoirs of nurse training in the 1970s* and *Hurry up Nurse 2: London calling*, Dawn worked as a hospital nurse, midwife, district nurse and community matron across her career. Before turning her hand to writing for a living, she had multiple articles published in professional journals and coedited a nursing textbook.

She grew up in Leicester, later moved to London and Berkshire, but now lives in Derbyshire. Dawn holds a Bachelor's degree with Honours and a Master's degree in education. Writing across genres, she also writes for children. Dawn has a passion for nature and loves animals, especially dogs. Animals will continue to feature in her children's books, as she believes caring for animals and nature helps children to become kinder human beings.

Printed in Dunstable, United Kingdom

66272344R00211